HEY! HE'S CHEATING!

Ryan stared hard at the pitcher's mound, trying to pick out the white of the pitcher's rubber from the dirt. It wasn't easy to spot. He finally detected a corner of it as the Baron went into his wind-up. The pitcher was throwing from a good foot and a half in front of the rubber.

"Hey! He's cheating!" he said, standing and pointing to the mound.

Art pulled Ryan down to the bench beside him. "Keep it down. Let's not make a scene."

This was the last straw for Ryan. How much was Art going to sit and take before something was done? . . .

Ask for these White Horse titles from Chariot Books:

New Kid on the Block
Satch and the Motormouth

At Left Linebacker, Chip Demory
A Winning Season for the Braves
Mystery Rider at Thunder Ridge
Seventh-Grade Soccer Star
Batter Up!
Full Court Press

Mystery on Mirror Mountain
Courage on Mirror Mountain

A WINNING SEASON FOR THE BRAVES

NATE AASENG

Chariot Books
David C. Cook Publishing Co.

To the home team:
Linda, Jay, and Maury

A White Horse Book
Published by Chariot Books,
an imprint of David C. Cook Publishing Co.
David C. Cook Publishing Co., Elgin, Illinois 60120
David C. Cook Publishing Co., Weston, Ontario

A WINNING SEASON FOR THE BRAVES
© 1982 by Nathan Aaseng

Cover illustration by Paul Turnbaugh
Cover design by Loran Berg
First Print, 1982
Printed in the United States of America
92 91 90   7 8

Previously published as: Batting Ninth for the Braves

Library of Congress Cataloging-in-Publication Data

Aaseng, Nathan.
   A winning season for the braves.

   Summary: Although at first Ryan and the other
members of the Braves baseball team are disappointed in
the strange coaching tactics of their new coach, they
eventually discover the benefits of cooperating and
listening to what he has to say about baseball, life,
and God.
   [1. Baseball—Fiction.   2. Christian life—Fiction]
I. Title.
PZ7.A13wi   1988   [Fic]   82-72711
ISBN 1-55513-950-7

Contents

1
New Coach

"It's not like he was such a great coach," shrugged Tracy. "I mean, how many games did we win last year? Three."

Ryan squinted hard at his friend. *This whole thing must have him really upset*, he thought. *If I'd tried to say what he just said, he'd be after me with both fists flying.*

"I don't get it," said Mike from somewhere behind Ryan. "I thought everything was all set and your dad was going to coach again, Tracy."

There were twelve of them sitting on a hillside behind a banged-up backstop. From a distance they looked like construction workers on their lunch break, except that they held baseball gloves in their fists instead of sandwiches. This was the entire roster of the Braves, a summer league team in Barnes City. Not one of them had been late for this first practice of the season. Every year there was something about that first feel of a solid infield, of a real dirt pitching mound, of a home plate that was stuck firmly in the ground and wouldn't bounce away when you slid into it, that made them want to play ball.

But now no one moved toward the infield, even though it had been empty for half an hour.

"My dad *was* going to coach," said Tracy. "Now he's not. All of a sudden he doesn't have the time. But what can you do? He said he was sorry and he even found a new coach for us."

Ryan had to turn his eyes away, for he knew how Tracy really felt in spite of his casual air. In Tracy's eyes it was just a matter of which of his dad's betrayals was worse, backing out of coaching, or going ahead and recruiting this new coach. His dad hadn't really asked who they wanted for coach; he just turned the team over to someone they hadn't even heard of.

Ryan tightened some loose strings on his glove and tried to keep from muttering out loud. Obviously it didn't matter to Mr. Salesky that the Braves had been counting on everything being the same this year. They had taken their lumps last season when they were the youngest team in the league. But now they were all back, older and more skilled, and they knew their teammates well. They'd thought there weren't going to be any worries or uncertainties this year because they'd been through it all last year. And now this.

"Hey, Tracy! Isn't that your dad's car?"

"Maybe he changed his mind!"

Ryan stared hard as the blue Vega picked its way over the rutted road that led to the ball diamond. His fists were clenched with hope as Tracy's dad got out of the driver's side. But they suddenly relaxed. Tracy let out a humorless laugh when the passenger door opened and another man climbed out. One of the two men was gripping a bat in one hand and straightening the whistle around his neck with the other, and it wasn't Mr. Salesky. No, Tracy's dad had on some pressed pants and a button-down shirt, the kind that men wear under suits. Even his shoes were shined. He wasn't here to coach baseball.

"Boys," he called. "I'm sure that Tracy, uh, told you what's going on with me. I don't know if you consider it good news or bad. I know I was looking forward to the summer because you're a great bunch to work with. But I'm just going to be away too often in the next few months to do any justice to the job." He had begun by looking each of the boys in the eye as he spoke, the way he always had. But their glum expressions must have caught him by surprise, because soon he was looking only at the man next to him.

"You've never met Art Horton, I assume, since he says he hasn't met you. But I've worked out with him at the gym and I know that he'll be an excellent coach." Mr. Salesky glanced at his watch. "Well, I am no longer the coach now, just a nosy parent. So I'll get out of your way. Good luck to all of you." He scrambled Tracy's hair, waved, and climbed back into the car.

Ryan wondered why Art Horton was standing up there with such a huge grin—a silly one, really. No one else had found anything to smile about. The new coach looked like a coach, dressed in a gray sweatsuit that was too tight around the waist to be comfortable. His mustache was so thick that it covered his whole mouth whenever he stopped smiling. He squeezed the bat in one hand, sending a wave of muscles rippling through his large forearms. Ryan could guess right away that this man was a good athlete, and it scared him. There was nothing scary about Mr. Salesky when he hit a ball to you in fielding practice. But you would have to really be on your toes whenever this man pointed a bat at you.

Nobody had said a word yet. The team stared at Art as though he were a stranger grinning out of a car window and offering candy. But suddenly the man's grin vanished, so quickly that Ryan flinched.

"Gentlemen! Front and center!" shouted the new coach. "Come on, gather around. Get in here close so I don't have to scream my head off to be heard!" Ryan jumped up automatically and joined the others as they shuffled forward. Tracy took his time getting to his feet, as if to do so were a nuisance.

Art Horton stood up straight now, with arms crossed, and he was not smiling. "My name is Art Horton!" he boomed. "You will call me 'Art.' Not 'Coach' or 'Coach Horton' or 'Mr. Horton'; the name is Art! Now listen up, all of you!"

Ryan edged behind another boy to get out of Art's line of sight. He knew from Art's first words that his summer was shot. There was no way he would stick around for this kind of thing all summer. As soon as practice was over, he would quit the team and never come back. What's more, he bet that he wasn't the only one.

"Can anyone tell me how many games you won last year?" said Art, with his lip curled up almost into a sneer.

Ryan could hardly stand to stay any longer. *He knows what our record was last year,* he thought. *He's just rubbing it in.* He looked hopefully at the sun, which was sliding slowly out of sight. At least this guy had been so late in coming that there wouldn't be much time for practice tonight. The sun was nearly down, and this field didn't have any lights. He tried to picture what he was going to do with his lost summer.

"What's the matter, did you forget?" challenged Art.

"We won three," said Tracy coldly.

"Good, we got someone here who can speak. And how many games did your team lose?"

"Fifteen," said Tracy. As the best athlete on the team, he knew that none of the blame for their poor record could be put on him.

"Fifteen games? Was that fun? Did all of you have a great time losing fifteen games?" said Art. A few mumbled noes followed.

"Well, let me tell you something, gentlemen," Art went on. "As long as I am the coach here, things will be different. Because I have one job, and you have one job, and we all know what your job is. My job is to get something out of you guys, and that's what I'm going to do. I'm not here to waste my time. If I want to do that, I can watch tv reruns with the sound off. Or with the sound on, for that matter. The reason you are here can be summed up in one word. I'll give you a hint: the word has three letters. Is there anyone here who can spell that word?"

Ryan found himself cheering the sun on, pleading for darkness to end the horrid meeting. He heard a couple of halfhearted voices spelling out w-i-n.

Art glowered at the team. "You have a strange way of spelling, gentlemen. I always thought you spelled fun, f-u-n." Suddenly he broke into a laugh. "Aha! I really had you guys going for awhile, didn't I? You thought I was Old Blood-and-Guts himself. Well, I'm only tough when it comes to one thing. Anyone who isn't here to *enjoy* the game of baseball might just as well leave now."

13

A dozen heads turned toward each other, looking as if they had seen an animal speak. Ryan caught Joe Martinez's glance, and nodded as he saw him mouth the word, "Weird."

"All right, everyone, line up on the first base line. Would you do that?" Art called cheerily. Before the rest of the team could react, Tracy jumped to his feet and stalked directly to third base, staring at Art every step of the way. Ryan nudged Joe and they joined Tracy at third, followed by the rest of the team.

Art scratched his head. "I said 'first base.' This can mean only one of two things. Either I'm looking into a mirror or we're really going to have to go back to the basics of this game! You, sir!" he said, pointing to Tracy. "I would like your assistance for a minute."

"Oh, boy, I wonder what he's going to do to Tracy," said Mike.

"I don't know," said Ryan, who was glad at least to be out of arm's reach of the new coach. "I do know one thing. This summer isn't going to be as good as we thought."

"Look, I think he's trying to get in good with Tracy," said Mike as they saw their star player talking into Art's ear. "I'll bet he lets big shot Tracy run the whole team, just so he can get in good with someone."

"Ladies and gentlemen!" shouted Art. "I will now introduce to you the Barnes City Braves. As I call their names, they will sprint around the bases and you can give each one a huge round of applause. Leading off is the world famous batting star, the only athlete ever to get a standing ovation in 113 different countries including Upper Volta, Joe Martinez!"

Joe looked around and hestitated. Art was pointing to the basepath and making a large circling motion with his hand. Finally, Joe dashed around the bases and Art led the startled team in a round of applause.

"Second up is the man who, just this season, was voted the toughest out in the entire civilized world, Bartholomew Smith. Yahooo!

"Third, the man who has broken all of Hank Aaron's records by the age of 12, Mike Sherry!" So it went, with Troy Williams, Al Rhodes, Dave Perlock, Perry Bradovich, Randy Olson, Jimmy Amadibele (Art had trouble pronouncing that), and Justin Holmberg each tearing around the bases while the new coach shouted some wild tribute to their greatness.

Ryan was the next to the last to be called, and for some reason he felt nervous waiting for his turn. Even though he was well prepared for it, the sound of Art booming out his name made him jump. "Next up is Ryan Court! Ryan is considered too good for the Hall of Fame, so they're building a special wing in the building just for him!" The image almost brought out a grin in Ryan, but he ran smoothly around the bases, shaking his head as if the whole exercise were too childish for words. Tracy took his turn last of all, and he trotted slowly around the infield, going the wrong way. Art ignored him and began dismissing the team before Tracy had finished.

"Gentlemen, that was just to get used to having our footprints on the bases. Next time we will start beating the stitches out of that little white ball and see if we know what to do with a baseball once it has been hit. See you then." He tucked the whistle under his shirt and jogged up the hill toward Lexington Street with that bat still in his hand.

Ryan headed for the bike rack where his ten-speed was chained together with Mike's bike. "Pretty tough practice," laughed Mike.

"Probably my toughest one of the summer," said Ryan, pulling open the lock and unwrapping it from their bikes. "I may just sit out the rest of them."

"Not a bad idea," said Tracy, joining them. "I can't tell if this guy is a baseball coach or a circus trainer."

"Oh, I don't know. After a while I think I started to like him," said Mike.

"He is kind of funny," admitted Ryan.

"Hokey is a better word," scoffed Tracy.

"Don't give up on the season already," said Mike as they rode, standing up, over the rutted path. Even though he wasn't resting on the seat, the jarring shook him so much that his voice wobbled. He stopped to inspect his tires. "Give it another practice or two before you quit and wreck your whole summer."

"I have a feeling it's already wrecked," Ryan said, slowing down. "Up until this we had it all planned out just perfect."

"Aw, I may as well stick around for the practices until I get totally sick of it," said Mike. "He'd have to be the world's worst coach to get me to quit baseball."

Tracy waited with Ryan for Mike to catch up. Tracy called to Mike, "Of course I can see why Ryan wouldn't want to play anymore. If he's too good for the Hall of Fame, how can you expect him to play with a team like ours!"

Their mission was a grim one and the faces of the three boys reflected it. Tracy's jaw snapped nervously on his gum, and Ryan and Bartholomew Smith walked with their faces scrunched in a frown. Smith told Ryan that he'd been quite willing to accept the new coach—until Art had used his full name, Bartholomew

16

Smith. Everyone had always called him "Smith," and if he used a first name at all, it was "Bart." But Art had said "Bartholomew," the name he hated, and now everyone was teasing him, calling him that.

The three marched in a tight group through Tracy's house to the garage and arrived in time to see the automatic door open, letting out a strong waft of gasoline. Seconds later, the blue Vega pulled in; the rumbling of even that small engine sounded loud as it echoed off the close walls of the garage. Then the motor stopped and the boys moved closer. Before Mr. Salesky could put in a word of greeting, Tracy started in. "Please, dad, I'm asking you one last time to come back and coach us."

"Please, Mr. Salesky, we're desperate!" Smith whined.

Ryan had been lagging behind the other two, and now he was glad. He'd hated the idea of putting Mr. Salesky on the spot by begging, but Tracy had insisted there was still a chance to change his mind. All that was needed was for a group of the guys to come over and show how important it was to them. But as soon as he saw Mr. Salesky's weary sigh, Ryan was sure Tracy had been dreaming. There was no way Mr. Salesky would coach.

"I know it's terrible to beg you," said Smith, "but you don't know how much it would mean to us!"

"I'm flattered that you think so much of my coaching," smiled Mr. Salesky. But when he turned to Tracy, his smile had vanished. "We've gone over this a dozen times. If I thought I could handle it, I would. But with the convention coming up, and the amount that I'm responsible for, and the time I'll have to spend out of town in the next weeks, I would miss too much."

"I know you're busy, but you promised and we were looking—"

"Tracy!" said Mr. Salesky, slamming the door. Ryan wished he could leave. As much as he wanted him for a coach, he did not want to make such a stink about it. "What more can I say?" asked Mr. Salesky. "It's not anyone's fault; it's just the way it is. Besides, Art's a better coach and a great guy, and you're better off with him."

"Art's a jerk!" said Tracy, knowing he was beaten.

"Listen to me," said Mr. Salesky in a low, even voice that had a tone of warning in it. "You don't have a right to say that about anyone. And especially not about a man you don't even know yet, who is willing to give up his time for you." He moved forward slowly, eyes only on his son. "I want you to grow up and face facts, and I won't hear another word about this. Art Horton is the coach. I am not. If you want to play baseball this summer, you'll learn to give him a chance."

Ryan did not know what effect that speech had on Tracy, but he himself could hardly keep from shaking. He felt lucky that his mom had never chewed him out in front of any of his friends. Just listening to Mr. Salesky's speech made him wonder why they wanted him so badly for a coach.

"I guess that's the end of that," said Smith after Mr. Salesky had gone.

"We really convinced him, didn't we?" said Ryan. "Now at least there's no question about it. Art Horton is the coach."

"We'll see about that," said Tracy as he stormed into the house.

2
This is
Baseball?

Mrs. Court stopped and leaned backwards around the hall corner, holding onto the wall to keep her balance. Ryan thought she was going to fall over. "Ryan, it's nearly six-thirty," she said, continuing into the den. "You're going to have to be quick if you expect to get to your baseball practice on time."

Ryan looked up from his tv show and recognized that furrowed-brow look of his mom's. Pulling on his jogging shoes he said casually, "Oh, is it that late already?" But he could tell by the smile tugging at one corner of her mouth that his act wasn't fooling her. It almost never did.

"Ryan Court, we ate supper early tonight because *you* have baseball practice at six-thirty! Are you trying to convince me that you suddenly forgot all about it?"

Ryan thought about trying one more denial, but he had too much sense to go through with it. He had been putting off this decision about the team and didn't want to tell his mom about it. It had seemed like an easy way out, at least for this evening, just to let the practice time slip quietly past. He turned off the tv with a touch of his finger. "I've been thinking about whether to go or not."

"Is this the same Ryan who was out throwing a ball against the garage wall before the snow had melted this spring? The one who risked facing an angry mother when he got his pants all muddy? You must be having all kinds of problems with that new coach."

"What makes you think that?" asked Ryan.

Mrs. Court sat heavily on the couch and rubbed her feet. "You don't have to be so secretive. No one's making you play baseball." Suddenly she frowned and said, "These problems with the coach wouldn't have anything to do with Tracy, by any chance?"

Ryan tapped absently on top of the tv and smiled to himself. For once she was wrong. "No, Tracy's got nothing to do with it."

"You're sure, now?" she said with a hint of suspicion. "It's not as if that boy's temper hasn't gotten you both in trouble a few times. I hope you've learned not to follow his lead when he gets like that."

"Don't worry." Ryan thought back to some of the scrapes they'd gotten into in the neighborhood and at school. He shrugged it off, thinking, *You can't be friends with a guy since kindergarten and not get into some kind of trouble together.* Then he repeated to his mom, "Tracy's got nothing to do with it."

"Well, all right. So if you're miserable playing with your friends, just don't go out for the team. There's no sense sitting around here stewing about it."

"But I'd hate to give it up for the whole summer,"

said Ryan. "What would I do with my time?"

"You'd probably just rot and be bored to death. But at least that's better than suffering under Ivan the Terrible on the baseball field."

"Art isn't quite that bad."

"Danny!" called Mrs. Court to her younger son in the next room. "Would you please bring me the footstool from the living room?" She turned back to Ryan. "If you're trying to convince me that you don't want to play with the team, you'll have to try harder. And no, I won't drive you. My feet are killing me, and I don't want to waste gas, so you'll just have to be a few minutes late."

Often after talking with his mom, Ryan found himself doing things without really knowing why. This was another of those times. He hung his mitt over the handlebars of his bike, opened the backyard gate, and sped off. His lower gears were slipping, so he had to pedal up the final hill to the school in a higher gear. It felt as though he were lifting leg weights. Finally, with a hard push, he made it to the top and let his quivering legs dangle off the pedals as he coasted down the parking lot hill.

He was expecting to see Art hitting baseballs to his buddies, who would be scattered around the grass ball diamond. Art was swinging a bat, all right, but Ryan could see only five Braves out on the field. Tracy was not there, and neither was Mike or Joe. Since Ryan had been in plain sight of the guys while coasting down the hill, he could hardly turn around and ride away. But there was no longer any question about his decision. He would not be playing for the Braves this year. "This is absolutely the last practice," he muttered as he chained his bike to the rack and trudged toward the field.

Suddenly a flurry of action off to his left made him stop. There on the blacktop, standing in a straight line facing the school wall, was the rest of the team. At a glance he could pick out Tracy, who was taller than the rest, Mike with his shaggy brown hair, Joe with his wiry build, black hair and red baseball cap, and Troy with his afro and glasses. They were all laughing and firing baseballs at some kind of poster that was hung on the wall of the school. Ryan veered toward the blacktop away from the diamond and saw that two balls were being kept in constant motion. As he drew nearer, the picture came into focus, and he saw that it was a blowup of a snapshot of Art.

"Hey! Ryan finally showed up!"

"It's about time!"

"Come on over! We're trying to hit Art's nose!"

Ryan whirled to see what Art's reaction was, but the coach was paying no attention to them. He was busy chopping ground balls as fast as they could be fielded.

"Somebody's got a lot of guts!" said Ryan. "Whose bright idea was this? And what does the coach think about it?"

"You're supposed to call him 'Art,' not 'Coach,' " said Tracy. "And I've got news for you. This is his idea, and he brought the picture." He scooped up a ball that had rebounded off the wall, and flipped it to Ryan. "You're suppose to aim for the nose."

Ryan stepped up the baseline and threw. The ball smacked the wall by Art's shoulder. Then a whistle sounded, and Mike trotted off to join the infielders while Perry moved over to join the "firing squad."

"Art doesn't like the idea of standing around at practice," Joe explained to Ryan. "He says the more time you spend throwing and fielding and hitting, the better you'll be and the more fun you'll have. So we keep rotating, with half over there fielding and the rest working on throwing accuracy. He put up that picture for some extra incentive. It's not a bad idea. Tracy's been knocking Art silly. The picture, that is.''

"And loving it!'' grinned Tracy, firing with all his might. *Smack!* The ball landed near the chin of the smiling face.

Ryan joined the throwers for awhile and then took his turn in the infield. He wanted to ask Troy where he'd gotten that official referee's shirt, but Art wasn't allowing much time for chatter. The infield was lumpy and littered with rocks, so Art was taking care not to hit the balls too hard. Still, when a grounder came towards him, Joe crouched so tensely he looked like a cat stalking a bird. The ball bounced straight to him, but took a short hop off his hands and trickled over to Ryan.

"What's the matter? You scared of it?'' laughed Ryan.

Phweeeeet! The piercing whistle made him jump as he was about to roll the ball back to Art. Troy had the whistle in his mouth and was pulling a yellow flag out of his pocket. He tossed it in the air and shouted, "Two-minute penalty for Ryan!''

Art signaled to Randy to take over at bat and keep hitting grounders. "Not too hard tonight,'' he cautioned. Then he trotted over to Ryan and pulled him out of the line of fire. "We'll wave this one off, Troy,'' he said. "I don't think Ryan was around when the ground rules were explained. Take a break, Ryan, and I'll tell you what we're doing.''

Ryan shrugged and bounced the ball to Randy. For a second he stared at Troy as if his friend had lost his mind, and then followed Art off the infield. It was the first time he had really seen Art up close and the mustache seemed even bushier than it had at a distance. He had worked up a sweat and his sandy hair seemed almost black near the ears where the sweat ran the most.

"You see, Ryan, there is really only one mistake that you can make in this game that's serious. At least that's how I look at it. That mistake is simply not trying. You can't get anywhere in the game, you can't *play* this game unless you try. Now, backing away from ground balls is fairly common among boys your age. Why? Because you're afraid that you might field it incorrectly. So the main thing I want to do is take away that fear of making mistakes. How? By not penalizing mistakes."

He pointed to four crude stakes that he had pounded into the ground next to the eroded path that wound down into the woods from the corner of the field. "I borrowed that idea from another sport. It's called a penalty box. For the first couple of weeks that we practice, we're going to have a team referee. Troy got the job for tonight, and that's why I gave him the shirt and the flag. Whenever he hears any criticism of another guy's play, he calls a penalty. The one who did the criticizing has to spend two minutes in the penalty box throwing stones into the woods. Oh, I know some of the heckling is meant to be in fun. But I want to see what happens if we play without having to worry about getting laughed at."

Ryan nodded dumbly and returned to the infield. He had been playing baseball ever since he could remember, but on this night he felt as if he was trying out a strange game in a foreign country. What kind of practice was this?

It certainly did not help matters when Art came up

with another set of rules for a three-inning scrimmage at the end of the drills. "I'll be the pitcher for everyone," he said as the team gathered around him. "Now, I don't want anyone looking for walks. Look for pitches to hit! What kind of game is it where you stand with a bat on your shoulder hoping you draw a walk so you won't have to use it? The fun of the game is in trying to hit. So, for this game, if you swing and miss at any pitch in the strike zone, it doesn't count against you. Got that? It's not a strike.

"In the field, all you have to do is touch the ball while it's rolling or in the air and it's an out. If you make the play, then it counts as two outs. Batters still take their bases if you don't make the play on them. The only difference is that your team is charged an out if the ball is touched. Each team gets four outs when at bat. Why? Again I ask, what kind of game is it where you stand in the field and hope the ball isn't hit to you? Try! *Play* the game! I want you as hungry to get your hands on a hit ball as if it were made of solid gold."

It took a good inning and a half before everyone finally caught on to all the rules. As the team's only experienced catcher, Ryan stayed behind the plate most of the time. He wasn't thrilled to see players get four and five misses before they finally hit the ball. "This isn't baseball," he kept mumbling to himself. When it was his turn to bat he hit a hard grounder that Jimmy stopped but could not field cleanly. Ryan easily beat the throw to first, but his side was charged one out because Jimmy had touched the ball while it was still moving. "This isn't baseball," Ryan complained to Troy as he took his lead off first base.

The climax of the evening came when Troy whistled two Braves to the penalty box on the same play. Dave had popped a short fly ball into left field, and Mike, who was playing in that area, started running in the wrong direction. By the time he finally located the ball, it was too late to catch it. He was still two arm's lengths away when the ball thudded to the ground.

Tracy and Perry let out a chorus of frustrated groans at Mike's misplay. Immediately Troy blasted his whistle and threw his flag. Ryan watched the two stomp over to the penalty box. He was so busy staring at them to see if they were really going to pitch rocks that he did not notice the game was underway again. The crack of a bat jolted him, and he ducked in panic. Fortunately, Randy had hit the ball in fair territory, and catcher Ryan dropped to his knees in relief.

By the time Tracy and Perry finished their time in the penalty box, it had grown too dark to see the ball. When Smith, over at first base, squawked about not being able to see a throw, Art finally called off practice.

"Sorry about that, Smith. I don't have my watch today, and I guess I got so carried away with practice that I forgot about the time. I promise I won't keep you guys so late again. Any questions about what we're doing before we go?"

"I've got one," said Mike. "How come you have the guys in the penalty box throw rocks?"

"A little mystery of mine," chuckled Art. "The secret is buried in the Bible. If any of you happen to have one and are curious, you can snoop out John 8:7. You'll find your answer there." Ryan was startled. Was this guy a Christian? But Art said no more and briskly scooped up the bats and balls and dumped them into the trunk of his station wagon. While the boys were starting to leave, he walked over to where his picture clung to the wall in three tattered pieces. "It's frightening the way you guys took to this drill with such enthusiasm," he laughed as he tore it down. "See everyone next week! Same time, same place!"

It didn't take long for the news about Randy to spread among the Braves at school the next day. It turned out that Ryan was the last to hear, and even he knew about it by noon.

Randy Olson was a big-boned guy who always seemed awkward, as if his joints needed a few turns with a screwdriver to tighten them. Yet somehow he usually managed to do well at sports. Last season he had been the only Brave to hit two home runs.

"I don't get it," said Ryan when Joe told him the news. "What does he mean he can't play anymore? What did he do, break his leg?"

Joe shook his head. "There's nothing wrong with him. All I know is that it has something to do with his parents."

"You mean they said he can't play anymore?"

"That's what I heard."

They were sitting at a lunchroom table next to the window, watching the rain beat down on the blacktop. Ryan had been thinking earlier that morning that they were lucky to have gotten their practice in on the night before the rain started. But the news about Randy made him wonder again whether it was any use practicing for this unlucky team. It was turning into a depressing day. The last days of school had really started to drag, and Ryan had the edgy feeling of just wanting to get the school year over with. It was hard to concentrate in class, and he felt like he did in those one-sided games when one team had to finish the rest of the game even though the other team already had it won.

Mike pulled up a chair next to them and poked around in his brown bag to get a preview of what he had for lunch. He took one look at Ryan and asked Joe, "What's wrong with him?"

"Oh, it's that bit about Randy," Ryan sighed. "That's just what we needed. With him gone, that leaves us with only eleven players. What if someone has to go on vacation or gets sick? We could end up forfeiting games right and left. How are we going to get through a year with only two reserves?"

"You're weird, Court," said Mike, biting into his sandwich. "First you tell everyone you don't think you'll stay with the team, and now you're worried sick because one guy quits."

"I want to play baseball this summer. But it seems like something keeps getting in the way," said Ryan.

"Don't complain," said Joe. "Think how Randy must feel. It's one thing if you decide you don't want to play. But when your parents tell you that you can't, wow! What kind of parents would do that to a guy?"

"I just talked to Randy and he said something about Art being the problem," said Mike. "You know, his dad was really mad about how late he got home from practice last night. But there must be something besides that. That's a dumb reason for making him quit."

"I wonder what else Art had to do with it," said Ryan.

"Who knows?" shrugged Mike. "Have you ever tried getting any information out of Randy? It's like playing twenty questions. I never met anyone who talks less than he does. Hey, Tracy! What do you know about all this?" he asked as Tracy finally emerged from the hot lunch line.

"You mean Randy? I heard Art blew it." It seemed

to Ryan that Tracy thought the whole thing was pretty funny. "The way I see it, Randy's out of baseball because Art doesn't know how to tell time," Tracy went on. "Well, I hope the great coach is proud of himself. Oh, excuse me, we're not supposed to call him 'Coach.' You know, my mom wasn't too thrilled about how late we got home last night, either."

"So Art lost track of time once," said Mike. "It happens to me all the time. I don't see why everyone's making such a big deal out of it. We're talking about twenty lousy minutes!"

"Yeah, I'd like to know what else is behind Randy's quitting," said Ryan. "I can't believe Randy's folks would come down so hard on him just for practicing late once. Maybe they know something about Art that we don't. But why would your dad pick him to coach if he was such a bad person?"

"I don't think dad knows him as well as he was pretending to," sniffed Tracy. "I think he just acted like he did so we would accept Art as the coach. Dad probably figured that was his best chance of getting out of having to coach us."

Ryan fired his paper bag into the wastebasket two tables away and got up to leave. "Great! So we're stuck with a coach that nobody wants, not even the parents. And we don't even know what it is about him that made the Olsons pull Randy off the team."

"If he had any brains at all, he would quit," said Tracy.

"You mean Art?" asked Joe. "I don't know. He seems like he goes out of his way to be friendly."

Tracy laughed as he poked at his hot dish with a fork. "You always have to watch out for people who try too hard to make friends."

3
The Last Straw

As usual, the Barnes City public pool was not opened until a couple of weeks after the warm weather arrived. Opening day was always a big event because this was no ordinary pool. It was more like a rectangular lake surrounded by a cement beach. Three lifeguard towers were spaced to patrol the entire half-block-long stretch of water. Besides being opening day, it was sunny and hot out, and as a result, even this huge pool was packed. Ryan found it impossible to swim in a straight line for long and had to weave around people like a slalom skier.

Ryan, Tracy, and Mike had each brought a younger brother to the pool. Those little guys always stayed until closing time, plus whatever extra minutes they could squeeze from the lifeguards with their pleading. But the older boys had swum their fill by midafternoon. They toweled off, put on T-shirts and shoes, and headed for the Burger House to fill the time until their brothers were done.

Mike pushed open the glass doors, which were covered with sticky fingerprints at about waist height, where small hands had touched them. But he stopped so suddenly that Ryan caught his chin on the back of Mike's head. "Don't look now," Mike started to whisper. But it was too late.

"Hey, guys!" called Art. "Come over and join me for a few minutes. There is something I want to discuss with you."

As far as Ryan was concerned, when an adult wanted to discuss something, it usually meant trouble. Tracy must have been thinking the same thing because he tried to back out the door. But Ryan and Mike had already shrugged and were walking over to Art's booth. Tracy pretended to pull a stone from his shoe and then followed them.

Art insisted that they first go ahead and order whatever it was they had come to buy, so the three of them waited in line for ice-cream cones. The coach must have long finished whatever he had been eating, if anything, because there weren't even crumbs on his table when the boys sat down next to him. A blinding glare washed over Ryan as he sat, and he wished Art could have found a spot that was out of the sun.

"How is the pool today?" asked Art. "And please don't tell me that it's wet."

The boys said nothing for a few seconds. Art had caught them by surprise, and they didn't know who should be their spokesman.

"Crowded and noisy," said Ryan, finally.

"But not bad," Mike added. "It's a good day for a swim."

"Say, I've been wanting to talk to you about a situation we have. I've been hearing some talk that Randy

31

Olson isn't going to play for us anymore, and I noticed he wasn't at our last practice."

"Yeah, I heard he was quitting," said Tracy. "How come?" Ryan thought he detected a nasty glint in his friend's expression. Whenever Tracy had that tight squint, it meant he was up to no good.

Art rubbed a corner of his eye as if he was trying to get out a piece of dirt. "I don't know. I hadn't gotten to know Randy at all yet. In fact, I was hoping you guys might know more about it than I do."

"His parents made him, that's about all I know," said Mike. "Randy doesn't say much about it. Or about anything else for that matter."

"Parents?" Art seemed surprised, but then quickly dismissed the subject with a wave of his hand. "Well, I didn't ask you over here to guess about Randy's reasons. But if he is serious about quitting, then that leaves us with only eleven players. That may cause problems."

"Yeah, I thought of that," said Ryan.

"Fortunately," smiled Art, "we may be able to make a bad situation work out for the best. At the church I go to, I met a family who moved into town about a month ago. They have a boy, Brad Chadwick, who happens to be your age and would very much like to play ball. Now this could be a perfect match. Our team needs a player; Brad doesn't know anyone and needs a team. I understand he lives pretty close to you fellas over on Basswood Avenue. So what do you think? Should I invite him to the next practice?"

"That depends. Is he any good?" asked Tracy.

Art laughed loudly. "Always a practical man, aren't you, Tracy? You've got a good business head on you. To be honest, I don't have the slightest idea what kind of player he is. But then we aren't asking anyone to be a superstar. We just want a good effort, and I think he can give us that. He might seem kind of awkward or out of place at first, of course. It's never easy to be an outsider breaking into a group.''

That last statement struck a guilty nerve in Ryan. He wondered if Art was thinking about the cool reception the team had been giving him. But the coach gave no clues as to what he was thinking. He just kept up his good-natured smile and asked, ''So what do you think?''

''Sounds OK to me,'' said Mike.

''Yeah, sure,'' Tracy said quickly. ''Well, we got to run. The pool should be closing soon, and we have to pick up our little brothers.''

But no sooner had they stepped outside than Tracy added, ''That really burns me!''

Mike swept back his brown hair, which always fell into his eyes when it dried after swimming. ''What's the big deal? We need another player. It won't hurt to give the new kid a break.''

''What about Randy? Nobody gave him a break!'' Tracy had deepset eyes to begin with, and when he spoke now they seemed to be dark, razor-thin slits.

''But there isn't anything we can do about Randy,'' said Ryan, trying to calm him.

Now that they were well out of range of the Burger House, Tracy was raising his voice. ''Notice who couldn't care less that Randy had to quit! Something dirty is going on here. First, Randy has to quit because of something Art did, and Art just acts like that's fine with him. Then all of a sudden he happens to have this new guy ready to take Randy's place!''

Both Ryan and Mike stopped walking as they let this

new thought run through their minds. It was funny how Tracy could turn things around. Ryan had not been thinking that way at all. He figured the new boy would be a nuisance, one more new thing he would have to get used to this baseball season. But he had also sensed that another player was probably a good idea. And Art was looking out for some kid he didn't even know. Someone who would do that probably wasn't such a bad guy. It had only taken seconds for Tracy to wash all that away.

"He's wrecking the whole summer!" Tracy was going on. "It's like he had it all planned that way. He would probably be happy to be rid of us all so he could have everything his own way!"

"Yeah," said Mike. "He does seem to be acting kind of suspicious."

"I'm getting tired of this," Ryan moaned. "All I want to do is play baseball. All right, so this deal stinks. Art may be a crook for all I know, but what can you do about it besides quit? Nothing. And if you quit, you can't play baseball."

"I told you before, I'm figuring out a way to fix all this," said Tracy as they reached the pool.

Ryan turned away from the other two and walked down the wet concrete path to the shallow end of the pool. Suddenly irritable, he wondered why it had to be his brother who was such a brat about leaving. The swimming period had ended, but Danny was still standing in the water, driving the lifeguards crazy with his begging. One of them finally threatened never to let him back in the pool if he was still there at the count of three. Danny scrambled out as if he had just seen a shark in the water.

Ryan hardly paid attention to Danny as the two

34

waved good-bye to the Salesky boys and biked the final three blocks home. He was starting to feel strongly that he just wanted to play this summer, for Art or anybody. It didn't matter who. Now it seemed that it was Tracy, not Art, standing in the way of a peaceful summer. "God, don't let Tracy do something dumb. Or Art either," he whispered.

"What did you say?" hollered Danny, pumping his pedals hard in an effort to keep up with Ryan.

"Oh, nothing. I was just thinking about the Braves."

"Tracy doesn't like your new coach, does he?" puffed Danny.

"You keep quiet about that. Just don't say anything to anyone." The more Ryan thought about it, Art didn't seem like such a bad coach. Maybe he was a little pushy and a little strange. But he seemed to like coaching, and he always had time for it. That was one big difference between Art and Mr. Salesky. Art never acted as if he had something more important to get to. But Ryan did not want to take sides against Tracy, either. Tracy sometimes had a big head when it came to sports, but he wasn't really a bad friend.

Maybe they can finally patch things up, Ryan wished. *Maybe the new guy will fit in fine, and there won't be any trouble and we can get on with the season.*

Ryan could not have been more wrong. Joe Martinez's throwing arm saw to that. It all happened right in front of Ryan at the next practice. Ryan could only stand by helplessly as if he was watching a runaway car roll down a hill toward a house.

At first everything had gone fairly smoothly. School was out now, and all the guys seemed to have settled into a more relaxed mood. The players were getting used to Art, and he had most of them laughing with his chatter as he pitched batting practice. Art sent a rapid-fire stream of pitches to the plate, twenty to a batter, and each served up with some kind of comment.

"Here you go, Smith. A nice, juicy one just begging to be hit!"

"Swing easy, Ryan. That apartment building is only a quarter mile away, and we don't want to break any windows."

"That's the way to knock the shine off the ball, Perry."

"Easy on my ego, Tracy. Be a sport and miss one for a change."

Tracy had shown no signs of the bitterness he had held towards Art. All had gone surprisingly well with the new boy as well. Brad certainly was no Randy; he probably spoke more words in the first half hour than most of them had heard from Randy in a year. He was almost as tall as Tracy, which meant he was a good deal taller than the rest of the team, and he was fairly heavyset. His efforts at blending in with the team were not helped by his bright red hair and freckles. Still, no one went out of their way to be nasty to him.

Ryan knew that Mike and Smith were watching the newcomer more closely than most as he went through the batting drills. Those two were the top reserves on the team last season. Only Justin had played less. With Randy gone, that meant a starting spot would open up for one of them—unless, of course, Brad took it.

By the end of batting practice Ryan knew they were out of luck. Brad was no slugger, but he was good enough to beat them out of a starting job. It didn't seem to bother Mike that much, but Smith was far more self-conscious about his lack of skill, and he moped through several practice drills.

Although most of the Braves thought they knew what the opening game lineup would be, Art never spoke about positions or lineups. Except for Ryan, who was the only one who was interested in playing catcher, all the rest took a try at each position during fielding drills. It was not until this final practice was nearly over that Art finally got around to the most important position of all. "Who's interested in being a pitcher?"

Most of the Braves thought it was a silly question. It was only natural that their star player, Tracy, did the pitching. He had pitched every inning of every game for them the year before. No one else even moved while Tracy stepped to the mound where Art was waiting for him. Art waved the others over to their fielding and throwing drills, and asked Ryan to stay and catch Tracy's pitches.

Eager to show Art what he could do, Tracy wound up and fired hard. The ball popped into Ryan's mitt over the middle of the plate, and Tracy grinned proudly.

"Nice pitch," said Art. "But don't throw so hard until you get a few more warm-ups in."

Tracy rolled his eyes and deliberately lobbed the ball to Ryan.

"OK, I've seen high gear and low gear now," Art said. "Have you got an in-between speed you can go to for warming up?"

Ryan was glad Art was being cool about Tracy's smartalecky stuff. Tracy threw five more pitches and then Art gave him the word to "fire at will." Art encouraged Tracy on each pitch and when he told the boy to stop for the night, Ryan felt relieved. The practice had gone without problems. Maybe Tracy and Art could get along.

"Joe, let me see you over on the mound before you go!" called Art.

Like all the other Braves, Ryan had been so convinced that Tracy was the team's pitcher that he could not imagine what Art wanted with Joe. But then he heard the words that made him pound his floppy catcher's mitt in frustration. "Ryan, would you stay for a few more minutes and let Joe pitch a few?"

Ryan could not bring himself to look at Tracy. He could imagine that angry squint as Tracy tossed the ball to Joe and left the mound. *What are you doing, Art? You're blowing everything!* thought Ryan as he crouched behind the plate.

It was almost insulting for Art to have drafted Joe for this pitching tryout. Joe was a skinny boy with a dark complexion and black, curly hair who always looked as if he was ready to apologize to someone. He was almost too nice to be competitive. It had taken him all last season to cure his habit of ducking out of the batter's box as soon as the ball left the pitcher's hand. Joe was really quite coordinated when he got over his timidness, and it made it all the more frustrating to have him as a teammate. Sometimes he acted so surprised when he hit the ball that he almost forgot to run the bases.

As Ryan waited for Joe's first pitch, he felt as though he were being asked to humor his little brother. Joe had trouble believing that Art wanted him to pitch the ball, and he stood staring at Art and Tracy for the longest time. Finally he threw, and the ball smacked into Ryan's mitt.

Ryan was so surprised by the speed of the ball that he barely got his glove up in time to avoid being hit in the face. He pulled the ball out of his mitt and peered at it as if trying to figure out what was responsible for getting it to the plate so quickly. As he threw the ball back, he admitted to himself that Art really knew what he was doing. Joe must have developed his throwing arm over the past year and Art had spotted it during the throwing drills.

Art gave Joe the same lecture he had given Tracy about warming up before throwing hard. Joe nodded sheepishly and continued throwing. He had a strange motion, in that when he reared back, his glove hand swept the air in front of him as if clearing the air of gnats. When Joe finished throwing, Ryan was not quite willing to say he was as good a pitcher as Tracy. But he knew he was not too far from it.

Art patted Joe on the shoulder and called off the practice. "OK, fellas, the real fun starts at 6:30 sharp on Thursday. I want all of you to get to the diamond at least twenty minutes ahead of that. This will give us time to figure out which bench to sit on and important stuff like that." He grinned. "Remember we're playing on that field where we held our first practice."

Joe had not yet moved from the mound. Apparently he still could not believe what Art had told him about his possibilities as a pitcher. Brad finally jarred him back to reality by slapping him on the shoulder. "Quite an arm you've got. Glad you're on my side. My name is Brad. What was your name again?" Joe nodded absently until it dawned on him that Brad was waiting for something. "Oh, uh, I'm Joe."

Ryan turned away from the mound and walked over to Tracy. Although he had not actually heard Art say anything about the pitching situation, Ryan could tell Tracy knew the pitching chores were no longer his sole property. Tracy was squinting and clenching his teeth, and he stared at Art as the coach packed the balls and bats into his station wagon and drove off.

It didn't occur to Ryan to be sorry for Tracy or even happy for Joe. He was worried about the team. Tracy had been doing a lot of talking about Art before, but he hadn't done anything yet. This might have been the last straw.

Brad could not have chosen a worse time to approach Tracy and Ryan. But he had noticed all the boys riding off in twos and threes, and it reminded him of what Art had told him. "Art tells me that you guys live only a couple of blocks away from me."

Tracy squinted at him coldly. "Who cares? I'll pick my own friends. Come on Ryan, Mike."

Ryan went with him feeling terrible and worried that the summer was going down the drain again. As they walked their bikes over the blacktop, he looked back at Brad, who was standing alone on the ball diamond. Brad must have seen him because he gave a quick wave. Ryan thought about waving back. Brad had just been a convenient target for Tracy's anger, and hadn't deserved that kind of treatment, even if he was a loudmouth. But then Mike asked him what time it was, and he turned back toward his friends without lifting his hand.

4
Eavesdropping

It did not take Tracy long to come up with a plan. In
fact, Ryan suspected that Tracy had been scheming all
along but had never quite found the nerve to carry
anything out. Art's latest blunder, however, had
changed that; it was a declaration of war.

Ryan knew who was calling and why even before his
mom reached the ringing phone. In cold tones, Tracy
asked if Ryan could join the group that was meeting at
his house. He did not need to say more.

It was a tight fit in Tracy's bedroom, with Ryan and
Mike sprawled across the bed, Tracy in the chair by his
desk, and Troy and Smith on the floor leaning against
the wall. Ryan wasn't surprised that Joe had not been
invited when he remembered the scene at the pitching
mound.

Tracy outlined his case against Art while leaning over
the back of his chair. Art had said that Tracy had a good
business head, but Ryan thought he also had potential
as a lawyer. He had prepared this plan and this speech

thoroughly. First, he reported that he had talked to Randy and confirmed that Randy's parents had made him quit because of Art. As for the details, Tracy said that it was a family matter that the Olsons did not care to discuss. Then he went on about how unfeeling Art had been about Randy, lashed out at Art's "stupid" rules in practice, and hinted that the coach was trying to push new kids on the team so that it wouldn't be their team anymore.

"And now he's got it in for me." Tracy was speaking slowly and calmly. Instinct must have told him that the more reasonable he appeared, the less reasonable Art would appear. "He decided to put Joe in as pitcher instead of me. Why? What have I ever done to him? Didn't I do well last year, considering how few runs we scored? But now I can't pitch, and no one gives me a reason. All I want is a reason. Joe never asked to pitch; it was all Art's idea. Just look what that guy's been doing! He's going to mess up the whole season if he hasn't messed it up already. Don't give me any more of this 'Wait it out until we get used to each other' stuff! We've tried that, and it's only getting worse."

"What should we do?" asked Smith, glowing with excitement. Every so often Ryan couldn't stand Smith. He was the sort who loved to get in on any sort of conflict. Ryan guessed that his disappointment at seeing Brad take his starting position was making this all the more important to him.

Tracy slowly broke into a smile, as if Art were already boxed up and loaded on a truck headed out of town. "If I can count on you guys to back me up, we can have him dumped off the team in a week."

Mike and Ryan exchanged a quick, anxious glance that Tracy spotted. "Don't worry," he said. "We're

42

not going to do anything against the law. Listen. Our first game is Thursday night, right? Well, it's simple. We don't show up. I mean, *nobody* shows up for the game!"

"Hey, decent! We're going on strike!" said Smith, clapping his hands.

"Knock it off, Smith! You want the whole world to hear us?" scolded Tracy.

Ryan shook his head. "The only ones we're hurting by quitting are us."

"Oh, no, we're not," laughed Tracy. Although he had tried to quiet Smith, he was having trouble keeping his own voice down. "When Art sees that it's just that fat creep and him waiting at the game, he'll get the message. Those two will be so embarrassed they won't show their faces around after that. We don't have to quit for the whole summer. Believe me, it's only going to take one game and then Art will be begging us to let him quit. Then the new kid won't be hanging around anymore, and the best part is, I think my dad could take over the job now. He's almost done with all that traveling, so he can't use that as an excuse. And with Art gone, we can get Randy back on the team. It's perfect!"

Ryan was sweeping his hair with a comb, wondering how he was going to say what he had to say. Somehow he couldn't seem to work up a hatred of Art. Fortunately, Mike opened his mouth first.

"You know, some of the guys think Art is kind of fun, for an adult," he said. "How are you going to get them to go along with this?"

"No problem. I keep telling you this is perfect. All we have to do is let them know what's going on, especially the way Art has been ignoring Randy.

Besides, they'll see that they don't have much choice. If the five of us don't play, they won't have a team anyway. The sooner they go along with us, the sooner we can get this whole thing straightened out."

Smith suddenly stood up and puffed out his chest. "OK, fellas, the real fun starts at 6:30 sharp on Thursday," he croaked in his lowest voice. "I want to see all of you there twenty minutes ahead of time so I can figure out how to keep my act together."

Ryan had to admit that Smith could do some great imitations. Somehow, though, he did not feel like laughing.

What he did feel like doing was riding his bike, alone. When the meeting broke up, he rushed off to his house and jumped on his bike before anyone could ask where he was going. Ryan had to get away from everyone.

He cruised the streets, distracted by his thoughts so that he wasn't riding as carefully as he should have. Something was not quite right with this business of Randy. Ryan knew Tracy too well not to notice that. It just wasn't Tracy's nature to make such a big deal on someone else's behalf. He was just using Randy's predicament for his own ends. Not that he was totally selfish; he probably would have backed Ryan in a similar situation. But for Tracy to be doing this because of Randy, whom he didn't know that well?

Ryan was nearly jolted off his bike when the wheels ran over a gaping pothole. He stopped to make sure there was no damage to his bike, and then looked around him. He was only a few blocks from Randy's house. Why not find out for himself what Randy's story was?

The Olsons' house stood on a corner lot, with

44

sidewalk on two sides. Ryan pedaled around the side of the house toward the front door. Subconsciously, he noticed that the car parked in front was familiar—and then he slammed his foot on the sidewalk to stop himself as he realized whose car it was. It belonged to Art, and there was the coach on the front step. *Why am I always running into him?* Ryan thought. Fortunately, he was largely shielded from Art's view by a large spruce tree, so he stayed in its shadow.

Art was talking to someone through the porch screen. As Ryan bent closer, he saw that it was an older man with gray hair and glasses that he kept polishing as he stood listening to Art. Ryan wondered why the man hadn't opened the door for the coach. It wasn't until he heard snatches of conversation that he found it was Randy's dad, not his grandfather.

Ryan knew that he should leave them alone. But there was something about the tension in the scene that froze him to where he crouched at the side of the porch. The strain of eavesdropping was made easier when the screen door finally opened and the men moved toward the end of the porch nearest Ryan.

"I want to make it clear that I'm not here to question your judgment as parents or anything like that," Art was saying cordially. "It's just that we feel bad about Randy leaving the team. Most of the boys are pretty down about it. So I wanted to come and talk, to make sure it wasn't something that I or anyone on the team might have caused."

Ryan heard a woman's voice next, and she didn't sound any friendlier than Mr. Olson had looked. "It's a long, involved story, Mr. Horton. I don't think there's much point in going into it all."

"Don't worry about my time," laughed Art. "It's

not as valuable as all that. I don't want to impose on your schedule, but as far as I'm concerned, I could stay all evening—if it would help clear things up."

"All right, fella," Mr. Olson's voice seemed to carry a challenge. "You barged in here asking for it, so I don't see any reason why I should go easy on you."

"Fair enough," said Art. It didn't sound much like Art's normal voice. Ryan figured the coach hadn't expected such a hassle when he came over to visit. He was probably squirming in his seat, if the Olsons had even offered him one. It was hard to imagine Art uncomfortable, and Ryan almost risked peeking over the hedge into the screened porch to get a look at him.

"If you really want to know the truth, then," said Mr. Olson, "it does have a great deal to do with you. The reason, one reason anyway, that we pulled him off the team was because of how late he came home that night. There's nothing so important about baseball that boys have to practice that late and risk riding their bikes home in the dark!"

"That was dumb on my part," Art answered. "Let me explain—"

"Let *me* explain," Mrs. Olson broke in. "Randall is under orders never to ride in the dark."

"In the future, we'll be sure to—" Art began.

Mrs. Olson didn't seem to have heard. "About seven years ago, when we lived on the other side of town, our daughter Julie was out riding her bike one night. It was dark and she was coming home from a friend's house. She wasn't the careless type. She had lights and reflectors on her bike. But there was a driver on the road who wasn't watching. Some people have said he'd been drinking. He claimed he never saw her until it was too late. Well, it was too late, all right! For four weeks we didn't know if she would live through it. She finally made it, but not all the way. She's off at college, crippled now. She won't be able to walk the rest of her life!''

There was a long silence. Ryan was shocked. He hadn't known much about Randy's family—certainly not this. Finally Art said, "I'm sorry."

"We've been through all the sympathy," said Mr. Olson sharply. "I mean to tell you that we won't let it happen again."

Art cleared his throat a couple of times and said, "I really am sorry for that. It's no excuse, of course, but it was my first night of coaching, and I was having such fun I just got carried away."

"Do you get carried away with your preaching, too?" Mr. Olson snapped.

Ryan's conscience had nearly talked him into leaving until he heard this. Preaching? He risked a look into the porch and caught a brief glimpse of Art's puzzled expression.

"I'm afraid I don't understand."

"Randy told us that you wanted the boys to study Bible verses," said Mrs. Olson. "No sense denying it, I wrote down the passage right here. John 8:7."

Before Art could answer, Mr. Olson continued the attack, his voice rising. "We're not about to stand still while someone sneaks his religion on our boy. We've gone the whole route on this, Mr. Horton! Used to be in church every Sunday. But not now. What's the point? There's no God in heaven if something like that happens to a person as nice as Julie. Or, if there is, I don't think much of him. So we don't talk about that nonsense in this house anymore, and no one will force it on our child. That, Mr. Horton, is why Randy will not

47

play baseball this summer!''

Ryan heard the porch door creak open and braced himself for a quick sprint back to his bike. But Art apparently wasn't taking the hint, for Ryan saw only Mr. Olson next to the door.

"If I understand you correctly, we have two problems," said Art, more calmly than Ryan would have believed possible. "One, I was an irresponsible coach, and two, I was pushing my beliefs on the team."

"That about covers it," said Mr. Olson.

"Before you get rid of me, let me try and clear this up. First, let me apologize one more time for running practice late. If it ever gets close to being dark while we're still at practice, I'll take Randy home—I'll take all the boys home myself. May be a tight squeeze, but we'll make it.

"As for the other issue, I can't even imagine what you've been through about your daughter. You've been hit with some tough questions, and it's probably not in my power to even talk about them. I will say that I am a Christian, and that it's important to me. But you don't have to worry about me preaching. That's something the parents should take care of. May I ask you, though, if you think a person has a right to act out what he believes?"

"That depends," said Mr. Olson. The screen door clicked shut again.

"Well, listen: It's part of my belief that Randy is important, that all people are. You make him feel that at home, but I think that he—and each of us—needs to feel it from friends, too. Well, I promised not to preach, so I guess I'd better stick to that. All I want to do with the team is make a place outside the home where all the boys can feel they're worth something. I thank you for your time, and . . ."

Ryan did not wait to hear more. He knew that was his cue for a long-overdue exit. He walked his bike for a few yards back the way he had come, and then climbed on and rode off. *So much for Tracy's argument about Art not caring for Randy,* he thought. *I have to hand it to Art. He really tried. And this whole thing isn't really his fault.*

He figured that if he spread the news he'd heard, he might be able to head off the strike. But he knew before he reached home that he would not tell.

He didn't want to make Tracy mad. Besides, the whole thing would be too uncomfortable. No one among his friends talked about religion. Except for Mike, no one went to the same church that he did. The questions Ryan had heard from the Olsons about God were disturbing. Somehow he didn't feel he should be talking about doubts like that.

Worse yet, he felt he could identify with Art. Regardless of what the Olsons had said, he still felt the same way about God that Art did. What if everyone really did hate Art, after Ryan let it be known that he really admired the guy in some ways? Ryan didn't dare risk it. There was only one way Ryan could see out of this mess. That was for Randy to come back to the team.

But as the hours ticked by, no one heard from Randy. The first game of the season approached, and with it, a showdown.

5
On Strike

The same group of boys that had gathered on Tuesday
met again Thursday evening in Tracy's room. Joe Martinez was also with them, squeezing between Troy and
Smith on the floor. The fact that Joe would join them
showed how effective their one-game strike was going
to be. The entire Braves team, except for Brad, who
didn't know about the boycott, and Jimmy Amadibele,
who hadn't shown up, was sitting out.

The plan probably could not have been carried out
by anyone but Tracy. He was the leader of the team,
and not just because he could play better than anyone
else. When Tracy stepped onto a ball park or a basket-
ball court, he had a way of taking command. He knew
all the rules and tricks of the game and when he wanted
something done, most of his teammates figured it was a
good idea to do it.

By the time Tracy finished telling everyone his opinion of the new coach, no one felt like standing up for
Art. Ryan squirmed the whole time, feeling as though

his insides were boiling. Tracy's pathetic tale of how Randy had to quit the team because of Art was the clincher. That even started Joe wondering. Tracy further swayed Joe by insisting that Art had brought him to the mound that night just to cause hard feelings between them.

"Ha! I would love to see Art's face about now," Tracy said. The digital clock on his bed whirred and flipped over a new number. It was now 6:20.

"I'd like to see Brad's face, too," chimed in Smith. "That guy thinks he's wormed his way onto *our* team and then, *wham*! It's just the coach and him!"

Ryan pulled out a pillow from under the covers and leaned against the wall, cushioning his head with it. He shut his eyes, doing his best to ignore Smith. He had not come over to celebrate or gloat about this strike business. It was nothing more than a chore that had to be done before things got even more out of control. It did not strike him as funny to think about what Brad or Art was going through. In fact, he was worried more than anything about what his mom would think of this whole thing. He had not told her about it nor had he even told her that there was a game scheduled tonight. Sooner or later he would have some explaining to do, and he was not sure that she would understand. She had been after him before about standing up to Tracy and his wild ideas. Actually, one reason he was over at Tracy's was so he would not have to be around to answer questions in case the phone rang.

Just then a phone did ring, and Ryan sat up quickly. The room had suddenly gone quiet, making the second ring sound as if the phone were in the room instead of downstairs. "It's probably Art," laughed Tracy nervously.

All of the boys could hear the footsteps crossing the floor to the stairway door, and they knew the call was for one of them.

"It's for you, Tracy."

"Tell him I'll call back later," Tracy called, and the others tried to stifle their giggles.

"But it's Randy Olson, and he says it's very important."

The smiles vanished instantly, as if someone had turned them all off with the flick of a switch. Tracy stepped over Troy and wedged the door open just enough so that he could get out of the room. As soon as the leader of the strike left the room, there was a different feeling in the air. No one spoke as they waited for him to get back with the news. Several were fidgeting and Ryan knew he wasn't the only one who thought, deep down, that this strike was not such a grand idea after all.

It was a different Tracy Salesky who edged his way through the door a minute later, Ryan noticed. Before, he had been so excited that, even in that cramped room, he had been unable to keep still and had been grinning with complete confidence in his plan. Now he looked like a boy who had studied all night for a test only to find he had read the wrong book.

"Randy is back on the team again," he mumbled. "He called from the corner store by the park and said we'd better get over there quick or we are going to forfeit the game."

"But what about Art?" asked Smith. "I thought Randy . . ."

Smith didn't finish the thought, and Tracy had such a glazed look in his eyes that Ryan thought he had not even heard Smith. While the others sat waiting for

Tracy to decide what to do, Ryan sprang off the bed. It had not taken him long to see that the strike was over. Randy had been one of the main arguments for the strike, and now that reason was gone. "Come on, let's go!" he said, nudging Mike off the bed. "We've only got a few minutes. Tracy, can your dad drive us? We'll never make it in time on our bikes."

"Uh, I guess so. Yeah. I mean, I'd better ask," said Tracy.

"Troy and Smith, come with us. Mike and Joe, can you round up the rest?"

"Yeah, I think I can get my dad to—"

"Then let's go!"

If Mr. Salesky had been looking forward to a quiet, relaxing evening after having returned from ten hectic days of out-of-town travel, he was going to be sorely disappointed. He had thinned out the lettuce in the garden and was doing the same to the carrots when the boys charged into the backyard.

Everyone seemed to be shouting at once. Ryan finally got the other two to be quiet and Tracy blurted out that there was a baseball game tonight and that it was due to start in a couple of minutes. "Can you take us, quick?" asked Ryan.

No sooner had Mr. Salesky started to say yes than Tracy pressed the car keys into his hand and all four boys hurled themselves into his little Vega, pleading with him to hurry. Mr. Salesky trotted over to the driver's side and backed the car out.

"Oh, no!" he said, staring at his hands as he lifted them off the steering wheel. They were caked with wet dirt from the garden, and now the steering wheel was covered with muddy handprints.

"Please! We'll have to forfeit if we don't get there

now!''

The boys kept urging him on, and Mr. Salesky had to fight the notion of speeding and cruising through stop signs. ''Didn't you boys know you had a game tonight?'' he kept asking over and over.

''It's a long story,'' Tracy said finally above the roar from the back seat. Ryan and Smith had started shouting at cars in front of them to get out of the way.

Finally, Mr. Salesky had heard all he could take. He slammed on the brakes and pulled over to the side of the road. ''I'm not driving another inch until you stop acting like a bunch of fools! I don't care if it does make you late!''

Ryan wanted to scream ''Come on!'' and he could only keep quiet by holding his breath. It wasn't until he felt his lungs bursting that Mr. Salesky put the car back into forward gear and calmly moved back into traffic.

It's lucky we're up first tonight or we would have had to forfeit, thought Ryan as they pulled up next to the field. Randy was already at bat. Brad was there, too, of course, along with Jimmy who, it turned out, couldn't resist coming to the park to see if everyone else was really on strike.

The Giants' pitcher threw a hard pitch and Randy took it for a strike. ''Three is all you get, '' said the umpire when it became apparent that Randy wasn't moving from the batter's box. ''Next batter!''

Randy whirled around in surprise and trotted back to the bench. ''I was so worried about whether you guys were going to get here or not that I wasn't even paying attention,'' he said.

When Ryan finally drummed up the courage to look for Art, he saw that the coach was not smiling. Still, Art

54

got to his feet, sent Jimmy up to bat and approached Randy. "Don't worry about it, Randy. It's hard to concentrate when you're waiting for reinforcements."

"Ryan, could you come here?" said Art after Jimmy had stepped in to hit. Ryan was expecting the worst. Without that smile, Art looked older and, well, almost dangerous. Ryan saw those biceps stretching the sleeves of Art's shirt and realized he had never made anyone that strong angry at him before. He didn't like the feeling. He was working through an apology in his mind when Art held up his clipboard full of scratched-out lineups. "Tracy is up next, and you're to follow. Start getting your muscles loose so you don't hurt yourself."

Ryan nodded and ran over to the bat pile, glad to get away from those eyes.

It was obvious that little Jimmy had been listening to Art's advice in practice. He clenched his teeth and swung at all three pitches thrown to him. The only one he made contact with, however, was the first pitch, which he fouled back behind the Giants' bench. He too was out on strikes.

"That's the way to go up there swinging!" said Art, greeting Jimmy with his old warm smile and a pat on the back. "Glad to see someone's been listening to me. You keep that up and you'll have your share of hits before the season is over."

Mike still had not shown up with the rest of the Braves, so it was crucial that the next couple of batters get on base. If they made their third out, they would have to go to the field, and without nine players to put on the field, they would have to forfeit.

Tracy did his part by lining a single past the second baseman. Ryan then made one last practice swing and took his stance at the plate. He had watched the Giants' pitcher throw to Tracy and decided he could hit against him without much trouble. The pitcher may have been a big kid with a windmill windup, but he didn't get that much speed on the ball. Ryan let a pitch go by for a ball and kept glancing from the pitcher to the rutted road that wound down the hill past the apartments. What was taking Mike so long?

The next three pitches landed well out of the strike zone and Ryan flipped his bat toward the bench as he jogged to first base. When he stepped on the base and turned back towards home plate, he saw Smith coming up to bat. Smith was such a poor hitter that Ryan was ready to concede the game. Luckily, the Giants' pitcher had not yet found the strike zone and Smith also walked to load the bases. Troy then walked to score a run.

Still there was not a car to be seen on that dirt road. Ryan sighed heavily as he stood with one foot on second base and clapped his hands, trying to spark some hope in his teammates. They were down to their last batter, Brad. It didn't matter if he made an out or hit a home run. If Mike didn't come soon, Brad was the last batter, and the Braves would lose.

Brad waited on the first two pitches, and they were both balls. Finally the pitcher floated a much slower pitch in, and it headed straight for the plate. Brad waved at it and missed by at least a foot.

Ryan couldn't figure that out at all. From what he had seen in practice, he was sure that Brad was a better hitter than he had shown by that foolish swing. An outside pitch was thrown for ball three, and then Brad grounded a pitch down the first base line. It rolled near the Braves' bench, and Art scooped it up and returned it to the pitcher. Three balls, two strikes. Ryan saw that both Tracy and Smith were staring down the road, paying no attention to Brad. Still no sign of the others.

Brad fouled off another pitch, and then the Giants' shortstop ran over to talk to the pitcher. When he left the mound a few seconds later, he was looking at the Braves' bench and grinning, and so was the pitcher. The big right-hander's next pitch made it obvious what they had been talking about. They would walk Brad on purpose, and win the game by forfeit.

By this time Ryan was convinced that the Giants' pitcher was easy to hit, and it bothered him to have to lose to such a poor team. But Brad reached out and poked at the outside pitch, barely ticking it with the end of his bat. As the Giants' catcher chased it back to the backstop, both Tracy and Smith saw a car turn into the road by the apartments. "Here they come!"

The pitcher heard their shout and quickly went into his warmup. It would take the car a couple of minutes yet to reach the ball field, and the umpire would not allow the Braves that much time between batters. Taking no chances this time, he lobbed a pitch a good five feet in back of Brad. But Brad had figured out what the pitcher was doing, and he swung his bat anyway.

"Strike three!" shouted the umpire. "That's three outs for the Braves. Giants are up."

Smith was howling over Brad's crazy swing until Ryan explained to him what Brad had done. By striking out, he had made the Braves take the field. The umpire had to allow the Braves' pitcher a dozen warm-up tosses, and that would give the car enough time to arrive. Already it was drawing near, bouncing over the ruts.

Tracy walked over to the mound, but Art called him back. "You can pitch next inning, Tracy. I can't let you throw until you've had a chance to warm up properly."

Ryan looked on in amazement as Randy went to the mound. Art must have had him warming up before the game, when no one else showed up on time. Randy looked about as awkward as any pitcher Ryan had ever seen. None of his warm-up pitches were over the plate. But on the eleventh throw, Ryan heard the car doors open and some wild cheering from inside the car. Six boys tumbled out, running as if the car were due to explode in three seconds.

"Three of you come over here, and the rest just find a position out there that hasn't been taken," Art shouted. The team arranged themselves on the ball diamond with Tracy at first base and Mike at shortstop.

As the Giants stepped up to bat, Ryan saw Mr. Salesky walk over to where Mr. Sherry was staring wearily over the top of his car. There was a lot of nodding and head-shaking among those two.

Randy found no better luck throwing strikes to the first batter than he had during his warmup. He walked the first two batters without throwing a strike. When he finally got one over on the third batter, the pitch was pounded into center field for a double. Tracy kept staring over at Art after each ball that Randy threw, but Art ignored him. After Randy walked two more batters, Art ran to the mound and Ryan joined the conference. "Don't worry about the walks; you've saved the game just by being here. But you don't have to throw so hard, Randy. Let them hit the ball and give your fielders a chance to help you."

Randy nodded and began throwing much more easily. The strikes started to come. The Giants hit two more line drives for singles, and Randy walked one more batter, but the inning finally ended when Tracy fielded a ground ball and Troy caught two flies in center field.

It did not take long for the Braves to overcome the Giants' 5-1 first-inning lead. A double by Randy brought in two runs in the second to bring them within two points. Then Tracy went in to pitch and had no trouble with the Giants' hitters. They did not even threaten to score for the rest of the game. Ryan, meanwhile, hit a home run, his first ever, and Tracy singled with the bases loaded to put the Braves ahead. By the time the seven-inning game ended, the Braves led comfortably by a score of 8 to 5.

Afterward, the Braves dutifully lined up to honor the league tradition of shaking hands with the other team. Ryan waded through the long line of dejected Giants and then noticed that Art had joined the Braves' line. It had never struck him until then that, although all coaches insisted their teams shake hands after a game, he had never seen a coach take part before.

Mr. Salesky had always had the team crowd around him after a game for a few last comments, so the Braves automatically gathered around Art at the Braves' bench. There was not any of the usual jostling and pounding that came after most victories, though. Everyone was waiting to see what Art would say about their attempted strike.

"I guess we showed them what a well-organized team can do," Art said. "After the way you guys entered the scene they must think they just played a volunteer fire department." The boys laughed nervously, still not sure what Art was thinking. Ryan thought Art seemed more business-like than usual, staring at his clipboard as he spoke.

"Look, I'm not sure I know what this was all about

tonight," Art started to say.

"It was just a mistake," Ryan blurted.

"Really, it's all been cleared up now," added Mike eagerly.

"That's nice to hear," said Art, sounding as though he did not believe it. "I would appreciate it, though, that if there are some problems in the future you would talk to me about them. We don't always have to agree, but . . . Well, good game," he said suddenly. "I'll see you next week. Will someone help lug the bats and balls to my car?"

Mr. Salesky was beaming over his son's pitching performance. "You boys played well," he said. "Maybe later on someone can tell me why I had to set a land speed record to get over here. But for now, if you still have any energy left, why don't all of you scoot over to McGraw's corner store and I'll get you a treat?"

"Decent!" shouted Smith. Those who had bikes rode them while the latecomers trotted across the field toward the store. It would take less time for them to run there than it would for a car to wind through that rutted road.

Mr. Salesky walked alone toward his car, flipping the keys in his hands. As he started the car, he noticed one of the Braves still standing near the bench. He recognized him as the new kid, and shouted, "Hey, son! Go on and join them. I'm treating all of you!"

Brad started to shake his head, but Ryan had seen what was going on. "Come on, Brad!" he shouted with a wave. He called to the group of boys who were leaping and howling their way across the sparse grass of the outfield. "Hey, we can't leave out the guy who saved the game for us!"

Brad was not the fastest runner, and by the time he

reached the others, who had slowed to a walk while waiting for him, Ryan and Troy had finished explaining just how Brad had saved the game.

Tracy, who was always impressed by a good piece of strategy, said, "That was quick thinking. Not many people would have thought to swing at an impossible pitch. You know, when we figure up batting averages at the end of the year, we'll let you count that as a hit instead of a strikeout. Come on, let's beat dad!"

But as Brad huffed to keep up with his teammates who were congratulating him, his smile showed that, at the present time, he couldn't care less about his batting average.

The Braves were hoping to hear how Randy happened to rejoin the team. But no sooner had they flopped down on the sidewalk outside the store with their bottles of pop feeling cool in their hands than Randy gulped his down and headed for his bike. "Gotta get home before dark," he explained.

It took most of the week and a lot of stubborn questioning before the Braves managed to badger Randy into telling most of the story of Art Horton's visit to the Olson house. Ryan felt a little guilty about eavesdropping that night, so he acted as if the whole thing were news to him too.

Randy even managed to tell his sister Julie's story, and Art's reaction to it. When he finally finished, Smith asked, "So why did your folks change their minds?"

Randy shrugged. "They didn't say much to me about the Braves after that, but late last night they told me I could play in the first game. No, I don't know what changed their minds. Art did, I guess."

"It's not necessary. That's all in the past," said Art as Ryan tried to make a formal apology for the team at practice. "Maybe we know each other a little better now. I will tell you one thing, though," he said sternly to the group gathered around him. "I'm tired of being the target of all this abuse. From now on, you aren't going to have me to pick on!" Without another word, Art stomped over to his car and climbed in.

"What's he doing! Is he quitting?" whispered Mike.

But seconds later he was back, carrying a large, rolled-up sheet of paper. He worked the rubber band off and held up the picture. His huge grin was answered by the Braves when they saw that it was a shot of baby Ryan blowing out his birthday candles. His cheeks were puffed up as though he were going to pop, and his eyes bugged out of his face as he strained to douse all the flames. "Here is your throwing target for tonight, gentlemen. Aim for the cheeks!"

"How did you get that?" gasped Ryan.

"Mothers are wonderful people," he said with a wink. "Let's go, now. Troy, Ryan, Joe, Brad, and Jimmy, take this fine portrait to the wall and start throwing. The rest of you take fielding practice. Except for Tracy and Ryan." Ten heads turned toward the boys he had named. "I'd like you two to do the hitting for me for a bit."

Art stood behind the boys as they sent high, bouncing hits at the infielders. Tracy hit balls to the first base side and Ryan to the third base side. After a couple of hits Art said, "Keep hitting while I talk to you. Actually, I asked you to hit so we could talk without the others hearing us." Ryan glanced suspiciously back at him, then sent a hard grounder to Smith.

"I've felt a little friction between us since the first

time we met, and I admit it's partly my fault. I've got to remember to explain things more thoroughly. Keep on hitting. I'll be honest, I'm guessing that you guys are the team leaders, and that you had a big part in last Thursday's little drama." Tracy started to protest, but Art made a swinging motion with his hands while nodding at the bat. Tracy went back to hitting, but he said, "It was my idea, not Ryan's."

"But it's partly my fault, too, I guess," said Ryan. He was having trouble concentrating on his hitting, and missed the ball completely on his next swing. "I was the one who started talking about quitting on you in the first place."

Art stopped the conversation until Ryan had a chance to hit a couple of solid grounders. "Like I said, I'm not concerned about what's past, except that I would like to know how we got to that point."

"I guess it started when you dumped Tracy as pitcher," said Ryan. He figured he might as well be honest and get to the bottom of this. "He was the pitcher all last year, and he did a good job for a lousy team."

"Ask anyone; I'm the best player on the team," said Tracy.

"I don't have to ask," laughed Art. "I've got eyes. So you thought I brought Joe in to pitch just to get at you? Better hit one to Mike, Tracy, he's starting to look bored. I should have told you my two reasons. First, Joe isn't nearly the athlete you are, Tracy, but he does have a good arm. I've watched him throw against that wall, and it almost hurts to see my picture taking some of those hits. He might even be a touch faster than you. You know that Joe can't contribute as much with his bat or his fielding as you can, so it makes sense to let him use his arm. That gives him a better chance to enjoy a little success. The other reason is that I need both of you to pitch.''

"We only needed one pitcher last year," said Ryan. Since Tracy had cleared him of any blame for the strike, he felt like backing him up.

"Do you ever wonder why you never see me throw very hard?" asked Art. "I used to be a pitcher, but now I have trouble even bending that arm. That's what comes from throwing too hard and too often at an early age. Eighteen games is too much strain on a young arm, I'm afraid. It would be better for both you and Joe if you pitch every other game."

"Well, if I'm such a great athlete, why did you put me on second base for the next game? Third base and shortstop are where the action is," said Tracy.

"That may be true on the pro level," said Art, "but I don't think that this league is quite that caliber. My guess is that there aren't many boys who will get a bat around when they hit against Joe. Since most boys hit right-handed, that means most of the balls will be hit to the second base side."

Ryan knew how Tracy appreciated good sports strategy.

Tracy stopped hitting for a moment. "I guess maybe I didn't understand what you were doing."

"Glad we could talk," said Art. He took the bat from Tracy and held his hand out for Ryan's. "Your turn to field. Now that we have that straightened out, we can go to the next problem. When practice is over, I'll tell you why Tracy will be benched in game four, and why Ryan will always bat ninth."

Both Ryan and Tracy spun around, their mouths hanging open.

"Don't worry," said Art. "You'll love my strategy!"

64

6
Heckling Points

It took the Braves only two more games to match their entire win total of the year before. Following their opening victory was a 9-5 win over the Dragons and a surprising 5-2 win over the Rangers. The Rangers had finished first the year before, but apparently some of their best players had moved on to the league for older boys.

Ryan had clipped out the most recent standings in the newspaper, as had most of the Braves. It didn't matter that the paper printed only the records and scores of the games without mentioning names or details. That one listing, "Braves 3-0," was proof to the world of what they had accomplished.

There had been some wide-eyed gawks before the second game when Smith, Mike, and Justin were put into the starting lineup and Troy, Brad, and Perry went to the bench. It wasn't until the middle of the third game that Ryan saw Art was serious about having no starters, reserves or pinch hitters. Everyone took turns starting, and everyone got a chance to play several innings of every game. The pitchers were taking turns on the mound, Joe surviving a shaky start against the Dragons and Tracy throwing well against the Rangers. Ryan wasn't sure if it was the system or the winning that was responsible, but he could not remember ever having so much fun in league baseball.

He had not been on the field more than two minutes during the game against the Barons when he sensed this game would be different. Jerry Gordon and Chuck Brock were wearing black and red Baron T-shirts, and the sight of them brought scowls to most of the Braves. Those were the kind of guys who kicked books out of your hand onto the sidewalk and then laughed about it.

The Braves were supposed to be in the field to start the game, but the Barons did not allow them any practice time. They stayed on the infield, throwing the ball around, snapping their gum, and spitting on the base paths. Ryan did not even want to go near them.

Art was no help at all. He sat scribbling on his clipboard on the end of the low bench with its green paint almost completely peeled off. After a quick glance at his watch, he whistled the team to gather around him. He took a deep breath of air, as if savoring it, and then rubbed his hands together. "What a night! Great night to be outdoors and playing a little baseball. I envy you guys! Wish I could be out there myself."

"I wish you could, too," said Smith. "Then we could really knock the ball down their throats!"

"It's too good an evening for losing tempers." Art smiled. "Pay no attention to our worthy opponents. We're here to play baseball, not to get into a spitting contest."

Ryan laughed along with the rest. He could feel his

stomach settling a bit now that he knew Art was aware of their opponents and was not bothered by them.

Art then read off the lineup and grinned as he said each name, as if this player were a secret weapon about to be sprung on the opponent. Tonight's lineup card was full of erasures and scratched-out names, so it was obvious that Art had been having trouble getting it right. But the list he finally settled on was:

1. Troy — second base
2. Brad — left field
3. Dave — right field
4. Justin — first base
5. Smith — center field
6. Mike — third base
7. Randy — shortstop
8. Joe — pitcher
9. Ryan — catcher

All eyes immediately turned to Tracy. Never in his sports career had he been put on the bench to start the game, and most expected to see some show of temper from him. Ryan wasn't worried, though. Art had already explained his system of rotation to everyone. Although Tracy was not thrilled with the idea, at least he knew it was nothing personal. He merely shrugged, plopped himself down on the bench, and said, "Go get 'em, guys."

Ryan bent down to start fastening his catcher's gear. He had been catching for a couple of years now, but he still had trouble getting his shin guards strapped on so they felt comfortable. As he worked at them, he tried to fight off feelings of embarrassment for batting last in the lineup. Art had explained to him that, since no one else wanted to catch, Ryan would be the only one to play all the time. He felt it was only fair, then, to have Ryan let everyone else hit first. Ryan had to agree, but it did not make it any easier to bat in the position usually reserved for the worst hitter.

Ryan was not the only one feeling embarrassed. Tracy had never been shy about letting people know how good he was at sports. Now some of the Barons, seeing him on the bench, could not pass up the chance to hoot at him. "Hey! Big star's sitting on the bench now!" "How're you doing, scrub?" "Hey, scrub, you're an all-star at collecting bench splinters!" As the inning went on, the remarks from the Baron bench grew worse.

Ryan thought the inning would never end. Jerry Gordon even had the nerve to laugh at Tracy while waiting for one of Joe's pitches. Ryan wanted to take a swing at him, and he could imagine how Tracy felt. He wondered how Art was able to keep their star on the bench with all that going on. *Come on, Art,* Ryan said to himself after Joe walked Jerry. *Let Tracy come in. Give him a chance to shut them up.*

Joe escaped the inning without allowing a run, and the Braves trotted silently to the bench. Art was stroking his mustache and frowning as Troy picked up a bat and started swinging on his way to the plate. "Are these guys unusual or are there other teams in the league that act like that?" he asked.

"They're the worst," said Ryan, angrily bouncing his catcher's mask off the dirt.

"They're even worse than last year," complained Mike. "They must have a real zero for a coach. Look at him! He just lets them say whatever they want."

Ryan followed Art's gaze over to the Barons' bench. Their coach didn't seem to be a threatening man. He was small and heavy with wavy brown hair edged in gray. He sat on the end of the bench, leaning forward with his hands gripping his knees, and he didn't seem to hear what his team was shouting.

Art shook his head and said, "No sense in saying anything back to them. A big reaction is just what they want. Just pretend we're playing a team of chattering zoo monkeys." He patted Tracy on the knee as he said it, but Ryan could tell it wasn't easing Tracy's nerves. His friend stared over at the ground around first base, and his arms were crossed tightly over his chest. The Salesky squint was back.

As soon as Troy stepped in to bat, the heckling got worse. They shouted, "Look out!" as the pitch came in and laughed when Troy missed the ball. The pattern was repeated for every Brave batter, getting louder with each swing and miss.

When the Braves took the field after failing to get a hit, the Barons started in on Joe. They made fun of his arm, his nose, his windup, and his occasional wildness. They also kept after Tracy, who was still steaming on the bench. After allowing the first two batters to get hits, Joe got himself under control. He reared back and fired as hard as he could, causing a loud pop in Ryan's mitt. As the Baron batters were called out on strikes, one after another, Smith and a few other Braves started talking back to the Barons' bench.

"Come on, let's not get into that," said Art firmly as his team came in to bat. "Let's go. Justin, let's see you take some good whacks at the ball."

Justin had been afraid to swing the bat the year before, and a few of the Barons remembered it. Jerry and Chuck roared so loudly when he walked up as the cleanup hitter in the lineup that even their own coach slapped them on the arms and told them to keep it down. Justin bought himself a few seconds of silence with a long foul down the first base line before finally striking out. As he trudged back to the bench, he muttered, "That pitcher seems like he's so close."

The Barons' pitcher was a large kid, and Art nodded sympathetically. "Yeah, he's a big one, all right. Don't worry about it, though. You really gave that foul ball a ride. Next time you might straighten it out, and then he won't look so big. Remember, the better the pitcher, the more fun it is to get a hit."

Smith followed with a ground ball that the first baseman scooped up easily. Smith was out at first base and he kicked the dirt as if disgusted with his poor hit. But Ryan guessed that he was putting on an act. *Smith's probably thrilled he was the first person not to strike out,* he thought. *Oh, great! Mike's up now. Justin, Smith, and Mike. How's that for a powerful lineup?*

Mike gamely battled the husky, red-haired pitcher to a three and two count. He was one of the smaller players, and when he went into a crouch at the plate he offered a small strike zone. With two strikes on him he always choked up on the bat, almost as though he were going to bunt. While Mike waited for the pitch, Smith was still griping at the end of the bench. "That pitcher's so big he looks like he's throwing from only ten feet away."

Ryan did not like to hear about how fast or big a pitcher was. It just made batters worry before they went up to hit. But it struck him as strange that both Smith and Justin thought the pitcher seemed so close. Ryan stared hard at the pitcher's mound, trying to pick out the white of the pitcher's rubber from the dirt. It wasn't easy to spot, since it was nearly covered with loose dirt, but Ryan finally detected a corner of it as the Baron went into his windup. "Hey! He's cheating!" he said, standing and pointing to the mound.

Everyone was busy watching Mike foul off the pitch, and no one but Art seemed to have heard him. Art pulled Ryan down to the bench beside him. "Keep it down. Let's not make a scene."

This was the last straw for Ryan. How much was Art going to sit and take before something was done? That pitcher was throwing from a good foot and a half in front of the pitching rubber! "Come on!" he shouted at Art. "Look at his—"

"I know, I know," Art interrupted. "He's not staying on the rubber. Look, Ryan, I don't like this whole scene. That team is out of control, and if we don't keep our cool, then no one will." They both watched as the pitcher, clearly ignoring the pitching rubber, fired a pitch past Mike's flailing bat. "Here's what I want you to do. We'll let the umpire handle it. When you're alone with him between batters this inning, ask him if he would watch that pitcher's foot. Ask him only once. Tell him I suggested that you ask, and then don't worry about it. It's his job to enforce rules, not ours."

Joe was still firing strikes in the third inning and it was only three pitches before the first batter was out and Ryan had his chance. It was all he could do keep from yelling, but he turned to the umpire and said, "Coach wants me to ask you to watch their pitcher. See if his foot is on the rubber."

"Don't worry about it, son," said the umpire, marking down the out on his card. "Let's go! Next batter."

Ryan pounded his mitt in frustration. He wasn't too sure about this umpire. In his opinion, the man wasn't doing too well at calling balls and strikes, and now he didn't seem to care that the Barons were cheating. He bent down wearily and held up his glove for Joe. The Braves' pitcher threw, and Ryan reached out to grab the ball over the outside corner of the plate. But he flinched as a bat swung and smacked the pitch solidly to centerfield.

Had there been a fence on the field, the Braves might have held the hitter to a triple. But the ball bounced high off the hard outfield surface and rolled on as if bouncing down an asphalt runway. The batter was already crossing the plate by the time Smith finally caught up with the ball near the infield of the ballfield on the other end of the park.

Trailing 1-0, the Braves finally got a base runner in the third inning when Randy walked. Joe struck out on a pitch thrown from in front on the rubber. Ryan glared at the umpire as he strolled to the plate. Why wasn't he doing anything? One ball and two strikes were both thrown so hard that Ryan could not get his bat around in time, and he watched them go by. Then came another hard pitch, headed straight for the plate. Ryan swung but hit nothing, and he dropped his bat and walked back to the dugout.

"Balk!" shouted the umpire. "I've warned you already about staying on the rubber, son! Runner moves to second base and that's a ball, not a strike, on the batter. Come back, son, you're still up."

Ryan spun around in time to see the Baron coach charge off the bench at the umpire. "What are you doing?" he screamed. "That batter is out! Get him out of here!"

Ryan backpedaled toward his bench. He didn't know if he was out or safe, but he knew he didn't want to be anywhere near an angry coach.

"The pitcher's foot was two feet in front of the rubber, and it wasn't the first time," said the umpire sternly. "You tell him to pitch from the rubber or take the consequences."

"You're crazy," said the coach. "Their pitcher's been cheating the whole game and you never called it on him. Anyone who wasn't blind could see Darrin's foot was right on the rubber! You're ruining the game for my boys!"

Ryan instinctively dodged as a shadow flashed by him, but it turned out to be Art. "If you're concerned about ruining the game," he said calmly, "cut out some of the talk from your bench."

The Baron coach refused to back down. "You can't take it, huh?" he sneered. "Your little feelings get hurt?"

"That's enough!" said the umpire. "You play baseball by the rules, and you start playing it now! Any more of this and I'm calling the game off and reporting you to the league. That goes for both sides. Now, batter up. Let's see, what have we got? Uh, three balls and two strikes."

The Baron coach had started back to his bench, but he whirled as if hit from behind with an egg. "*Three* balls? Is that what you said?" He scanned the hill behind his bench and picked out a man in a suit who was sitting alone. "You, sir! What was the count before that last pitch?"

"One ball and two strikes."

"Mmmm, that's right," nodded the umpire. "Sorry, it should be two balls and two strikes."

"No, you said 'three balls.' You had the count wrong and we're going to protest this game. I'm reporting *you* to the league.''

Art stretched his arms wide. ''Think of the kids,'' he pleaded.

''No,'' said the coach, turning his back. ''You heard him give the wrong count, and we're protesting.'' It probably didn't help his temper any when Ryan singled to score Randy. By the end of the inning the hoots from the Barons were so bad that some spectators were getting angry. Art called his team together before they went to the field for the fourth inning. Tracy finally had his turn to get into the game and Ryan bet he was so angry he would wear a hole in the catcher's glove if he were pitching. But he would be taking Troy's spot at second base.

It seemed to Ryan that, for some reason, the tenseness was gone from Art and that familiar grin and twinkle of the eye was back. ''Don't worry about that protest they're talking about. That coach doesn't have a leg to stand on, and he'll realize it once he cools down. Look, I know how tempting it is to want to beat this team 100 to zip,'' he said. ''They probably deserve to have it happen. But we're not going to turn this into a war or a grudge match.''

''You mean we have to keep taking it from them?'' asked Tracy.

''Oh, no,'' Art laughed. ''We came here to play a game, and that's just what we're going to do. I think I've got a game that will turn their tactics upside down. Here's the deal, gentlemen. Every time you get heckled or insulted, it's worth one point. Troy is through for this game, and did a mighty fine job, I might add, and so he will keep score. Just raise your hand whenever it happens to you. Now, if you can pile up 200 points in the four innings we have left, you win the prize.''

Ryan was not impressed. "What's the prize?"

"There's a certain big league ballplayer coming to town to speak at a high school banquet. It so happens that we played together in college, and I know him pretty well. If you get your 200 points, I'll arrange for him to come to our next practice."

"Which player is it?" asked nine Braves at once.

Art let the suspense linger for a few seconds. "Tony Dalton," he said finally. No one needed to ask who Tony Dalton was. The Chicago right fielder had almost led the league in home runs the year before.

Joe had barely reached the mound when Ryan saw him shoot his right hand in the air. *I wonder how Art comes up with all these ideas,* Ryan thought. Already he felt as if some pressure had been lifted. It was great to see Joe laugh and raise his hand after each pitch and to hear the cheers from the fielders as the "insult" total rose. He looked over to the Baron bench and saw that, although the heckling was as strong as ever, the Barons did not seem to be enjoying it as much.

At the end of the fourth inning, Troy announced that he had counted 97 points, and Art led a loud cheer to celebrate. "You're halfway there, fellas. Keep up the good work."

By the time Ryan batted in the fifth, the Braves held a two-run lead and the Barons had quieted considerably. The Baron's catcher spat to the side as Ryan dug his back foot into the batter's box. "What are you morons up to?" said the catcher. "You must be cracked."

Ryan whistled to the Braves' bench and held up two fingers.

"Got 'em," answered Troy. "We're up to 134."

"Awright!" shouted Smith, who was leaning on

Troy's shoulder, helping him count. "We're going to break it easy!"

Ryan felt such relief at the turn of events that he felt certain he would smack at least a double. But he swung too low on a high pitch and fouled out to the catcher. Ryan pounded his bat until he heard the laughter from the Barons. The anger disappeared and he jogged over to Troy after carefully looking over the Barons' bench. "I think I got five at once," he announced.

He gave Tracy a pat on the shoulder as his friend moved up for his first time at bat in the game. The sight of the big second baseman seemed to recharge the Baron bench. Ryan wasn't sure how much of it Tracy would stand for. He'd seen him get into fights for less cause than he had tonight.

"Hey, chump, swing!" shouted the Barons as the first pitch came in to him. Tracy stepped back and glared at the catcher, who had shouted the loudest. Then suddenly, he shot his fist in the air and nodded at Troy.

Ryan couldn't contain himself any longer. He jumped high in the air as he cheered along with the rest of the Braves. *Art's plan is working!* he thought. *Even Tracy's having fun with it.*

Tracy clouted the next pitch to left field and raced to second base well ahead of the throw from the outfield. "You run like a chimp," said the second baseman. "That should have been an easy triple."

"Two!" shouted Tracy to the Braves' bench.

"We're up to 148," answered Troy.

But the total stayed at 148 as the Braves prepared to bat in the sixth. Their lead had stretched to 6-1 and the Barons suddenly were not saying anything.

"No way we're going to reach 200 now," Tracy said

to Ryan. "They haven't said a thing for the last five minutes."

"Maybe they figured out what we're up to and are trying to wreck our chances," Ryan answered. "I wouldn't put it past them."

"I can see these guys aren't cooperating anymore," Art broke in. "But I'll tell you what. I'm so proud of you guys that I'll get Tony to practice with us if you reach 150."

"Awright!" howled Smith.

"Now don't get so carried away that you're begging for insults," warned Art.

It didn't look as though the Braves would reach even 150. No one on the Barons' bench was paying much attention to the game any longer. Tracy came to bat with two out in the sixth. With Joe protecting a 7-1 lead, this was probably the Braves' last inning to bat. Fortunately for the Braves, there were a couple of Barons who couldn't resist some final barbs about Tracy's starting the game on the bench.

"Hey, scrub!" "Hey, benchwarmer!"

The Braves broke into cheers even before Tracy got his hand in the air. They were still celebrating when Tracy hit a home run. Ryan was there to meet him at home plate as Tracy sprinted in. "Way to go, slugger! How many guys can be a hero twice in one time at bat?" he said as he slapped hands with him.

As the mob of Braves stumbled over each other on their way back to the bench, Ryan saw a familiar-looking older man come over and shake Art's hand. The man had been sitting on the hillside along with the other Braves' parents since about the third inning. Ryan knew all of the parents who regularly attended and often took his own "roll call" of them between innings. But he couldn't quite place this man. It was not until after Joe had notched the final strikeout in the seventh inning and Ryan saw the man surrounding Randy with a hug that he realized it was Mr. Olson.

"Boy, that Art never runs out of tricks, does he?" said Mike, after they had shaken the hands of some quiet and confused Barons.

"He's smart. You gotta give him that," said Tracy. "I guess we could have done a lot worse for a coach. Look at who the Barons got!"

"Yeah, I'll take Art," said Ryan. He'd defend his coach against anyone now.

"You're not kidding," grinned Mike. "We're unbeaten, after all!"

There are more important things than a winning record, Ryan thought, though he didn't say anything to Mike. *That's the way Art feels, I know, and that's why I like him.*

7
First Place

The second they heard the front door open, Tracy and Ryan dashed across the living room. The newspaper carrier who had so routinely pulled on the handle jumped back in surprise as the two boys charged at him. Before he had a chance to drop the paper in the doorway, Tracy snatched it away with a quick "Thanks" and dove to the floor. He tossed away the outside section as if it were only a wrapper, and found the sports section. Within seconds, Ryan and Joe were flanking him on the rug, each with elbows on the floor and chin resting in his hands as they found the standings.

The Braves were listed on top, with a record of 12 wins and 2 losses. Directly beneath them were two other teams with the same mark, the Rangers and the Hawks. The Braves had been beaten by each of them in the past two weeks. The Hawks had first pulled them from the unbeaten ranks with a 3-2 win in eight innings. Then the Rangers had won their return match with the Braves 6-3. Tracy had pitched that night and had not had a very good game.

"Hey, look!" said Ryan. "They put in a bit about our last game. 'Tracy Salesky collected three hits to pace the Braves to a 7-3 win over the Cubs.' How about that? You're famous."

"Had to do something to make up for the way I pitched against the Rangers," Tracy muttered.

Ryan and Joe had seen what they were after, and they slowly rose to their knees. But Tracy was still studying the standings. "There's a list here of all the games left on the schedule," he said. "The Rangers and the Hawks play each other next week. One of them has to lose, and I hope it's the Rangers. That way, they'll be out of the running and we'll get to play the Hawks in our last game. Hey, can you believe it? If we beat the Hawks then, we win the title."

"You make it sound like such a cinch," said Joe. "We have to win our other games first."

Tracy ran his finger down the schedule. "Ha! We play the Jaguars next, and they're 8 and 6. After that, all we have left are the Pirates and the Rockets. We could beat them in our sleep."

"The Jaguars won't be easy," Joe warned. "We only beat them by one run last time."

"Well, don't worry about them," said Tracy. "It's my turn to pitch again, and I'm going to make up for the way I stunk up the game last time I pitched."

Ryan glanced down at the schedule and did some quick figuring of his own. "That means you're going to pitch the last game against the Hawks," he said, whacking Joe on the arm.

Joe frowned. "I think I'd rather see Tracy pitch that one."

"No chance," said Tracy, folding up the paper.

80

"Art isn't going to change anything around. In his system, it doesn't matter who we're playing. He just plays you when your turn is up."

"You can't argue with the way things have turned out," said Ryan.

"I just hope he realizes we have a good shot at the championship," said Tracy. "Chances like this don't come around too often."

"What are you getting at?" asked Ryan suspiciously.

"All right, I know Art's doing a good thing by giving everyone a chance to play and all that. And he's just crawling with ideas, and he has a good point about making the game fun. And I admit he was right about letting both you and I pitch, Joe, because it turned out that you're better than we ever dreamed. But say it comes down to that last game with the Hawks. How would you like to get that close to a championship and then have to sit on the bench for a couple of innings—and end up losing?"

"I don't know," sighed Ryan. "But I do know that Art's run things pretty well so far with his team effort idea."

Tracy ignored him. "I don't know about you, but I'd never get over it. Do you know what it means to win the championship? We would go on to the regional tournament, and then we'd be just two games away from going to state!"

"Is that state tournament a pretty big deal?" asked Joe.

"Is it?" laughed Tracy. "Just think of it. A trip down to Charlesburg. We'd stay in a motel with a pool, and eat at fancy restaurants. Probably get to see the capitol building. They'd let us play on one of their best fields with fences and a grandstand. Who knows, we'd probably get our pictures in the paper along with some big articles, and we'd be famous around town. My dad says it's been twelve years since a team from Barnes City ever made it to state.''

The whole description made Joe so nervous he couldn't sit still. He excused himself and ran home. Ryan had not known about all that went with winning a championship, and he had to admit it sounded better than anything he had ever hoped for. He pictured himself hitting a ball over a real fence, and seeing a crowd stand up and cheer as he rounded the bases, hearing someone boom his name over the loudspeaker. *Batting ninth for the Braves is Ryan Court. . . .*

''Think of it,'' he said aloud. ''First Art brought Tony Dalton to one of our practices, showing us how to hit, and then we get a chance to go down to Charlesburg and play in the big time, all in the same year. How do you know all this stuff about the tournament, anyway?''

''If you read the sports section, you find out lots of things,'' Tracy said. ''Last year a team from Red Prairie won the tournament, and they got to ride through their town on a fire engine with a police escort.''

''Yeah, it sure would be nice,'' said Ryan. All this talk was starting to get him excited and the Hawk game was still two weeks away.

''I just hope Art realizes how important it is to go all out for that Hawk game,'' Tracy said.

''It's not like he hasn't given everyone lots of chances to play all year long,'' reasoned Ryan. ''Maybe for a game that important he might change his system a bit.'' Suddenly he got up and went to the door. ''Aw, who are we trying to kid? Art isn't going to change. You know how he always plays down the winning angle. By the way, what time is practice tonight?''

"Seven. He said it would only take forty-five minutes.''

No sooner had everyone arrived at the ball field than a small cluster of boys walked up to Art. Mike led the way and Ryan could tell he had something important to say. It made him a little nervous, because Mike was one guy who would say whatever came into his mind. Justin and Smith walked behind slowly, as if Mike was dragging them by a rope. The closer they got to Art, the more Smith tried to lag behind as if he were not part of the group.

"Art, some of us have been talking about the season and the standings, and it seems we're in pretty good shape for a championship,'' said Mike loudly. Obviously, this little speech was meant for all the Braves to hear.

"Yes, well, those things sometimes happen in life. I guess we just have to learn to live with it,'' Art answered in a mock serious tone. "Seriously, though, the whole team has done well, and I'm proud of you. Every single person on this team is playing the game and looking like he's having fun doing it. When that happens, you're bound to have a little success as well. And a little success is like sugar: it helps make things a bit sweeter.''

"We know,'' said Mike. "I think all of us appreciate your system and the good job of coaching you've done. We've learned a lot, and I think most of us would have liked playing this way this season even if we weren't leading the league.''

"Tied for the lead,'' corrected Tracy.

"All right, Mike. What's on your mind?'' laughed

Art. "When people start telling me how wonderful I am, I get suspicious."

"The three of us have talked it over, and we realize that the Braves are very close to winning the title. And we've kind of decided that it wouldn't bother us if you switched the system some. You could put the best players in for the tougher games."

Art stared at Mike as if he were trying to crack a code. "Is this your idea, or has someone else been putting ideas into your head?"

Ryan was wondering the same thing, and he nudged Tracy. But Tracy shook his head and shrugged his shoulders.

"No one said anything," Mike said. "The three of us have been talking. You made this into a good team, and we feel we're a big part of it. We want to do whatever we can to help the team. If that means sitting out a game or two, well, we've gotten more playing time this year than last year."

"Who decided that you three aren't as good as the rest?" challenged Art. Despite his coach's seriousness, Ryan had to choke back a laugh. For Smith was glaring at Mike as if to say, "Yeah, who put me in with you scrubs, anyway?" No wonder Smith had been trying to hang back in the shadows. He still really thought he was better than many of the players on the team. *I wonder how Mike talked Smith into going along with this,* Ryan thought.

"I think everyone on the team knows who the better players are," said Mike stubbornly.

Art pulled off his baseball cap and smoothed the hair on the back of his head. "OK, I'm not going to mislead you and say that the three of you are all-league candidates. At least not this year. But you've all improved tremendously since the first time I saw you play. You guys have added a lot to this team. You've played the game as hard as anyone here, and that's the only thing that counts, remember? That effort has paid off for you. Come on, each one of you has gotten some good hits this year and I'm not ashamed to have any of you out in the field playing your positions.

"As for this championship talk, that isn't the main thing we're here for. I'm not going to sacrifice any of you, or anything I believe in, to win. You start doing that and pretty soon baseball isn't a game anymore. The pressure gets greater and you start being afraid to go out and have any fun. I keep telling you, success is like sugar. A little tastes great, but too much can make you sick."

Art looked over at Randy standing close by and poked him in the stomach. "I promised I wouldn't preach at you, and now listen to me. Let's just keep doing what we've been doing, and enjoy ourselves, and we may even win a championship. And *you* might get the winning hit," he said, pointing a finger two inches from Mike's nose.

Ryan figured that was the end of it, but Mike wasn't taking no for an answer. "There are others with a better chance of that. You know we have two tough teams and two easy ones left on our schedule. We can still keep the system of equal time for all. Just put us in against the Pirates and Rockets and make sure Tracy and Randy get in against the Jaguars and Hawks."

Mike glanced around for support and Justin finally backed him up. "It would probably be more fun that way, anyhow. I'd rather play the Pirates and Rockets. At least I have a better chance of getting a hit off them."

Ryan thought back to the evening when Justin hit a double. *He's right, that was against the Pirates the first time,* he thought. Mike's argument was making more and more sense to him.

Art smiled but shook his head. "I don't know. You're getting away from the fun of challenges. If you start shying away, then you're spoiling everything we've tried to do so far."

"But we're not backing away," said Mike. "Give us a chance to help win our two games and give them a chance to win their two. We get equal playing time, we're both helping the team, and we both get our own challenge."

"We'll see," Art said, shaking his head. "I'll give the three of you credit for a very noble offer but, you see, I'm an old guy and I'm kind of set in my ways."

He hobbled as if arthritic over to his station wagon and struggled to get the hatchback open. "I'll admit your request caught me by surprise. Well, I don't like to be outsurprised by you young whippersnappers, so I brought one of my own. According to some of your parents, it's about time we had a dress code on this team. From now on I'm going to get tough on you and insist that you all wear one of these to our games."

With that he pulled open his shirt like Clark Kent changing into Superman, and there on his chest was a white T-shirt with "Braves" written on it in red. He then passed out shirts and Ryan examined more closely the red stripes down the sleeves and the piping around the lettering. "Look at these!" he shouted to Tracy, who needed no urging to do just that. "Wow! And pants and caps, too!" Art had pulled open a box of caps, each with a *B* stamped on the front.

"Thank your parents for the funds," said Art. "And

make sure that when you wear it at our games, the word *Braves* is on the front. Like I said, it's a very strict dress code.''

No more was said about Mike's idea.

The Jaguars were the best hitting team the Braves had faced all year. They probably would have run away with the league title if they had found someone who could pitch as well as they hit. As Ryan caught Tracy's warm-ups, he was wishing that Joe could be pitching this game. Joe had gotten better with each outing, while Tracy was starting to have trouble getting batters out. Ryan had heard Art tell Tracy several times to quit trying so hard and relax. He wondered if Tracy was trying too hard to top Joe's performances.

Art had stuck to his system. Tracy was on the mound, and both Mike and Smith were starting in the outfield. Smith had already just missed being hit by two practice balls while admiring his new shirt. Ryan hoped he could pay more attention to the game once it started.

The Jaguars were eager to hit against Tracy. Although they had lost to the Braves earlier in the year, they had scored six runs off him, and were confident they could get even more this game. Ryan could tell that by the look in their eyes as they watched Tracy warm up. There wasn't much chatter among the Jaguars; they stepped to the plate quickly and never took their eyes off the pitcher.

It didn't take long before Ryan realized Tracy was in trouble. The first pitch bounced three feet in front of the plate and skipped past Ryan all the way to the backstop. When Tracy did get the ball over the plate, the Jaguar hitters pounded it. After the first batter walked, there was a single, a single, and a triple in rapid succession, and each crack of the bat sent new pains through Ryan's stomach. Then Mike misplayed a fly ball and threw it wildly over Brad's head at second base.

At the end of the inning, the Braves sprinted toward their bench like people caught in a rainstorm dashing for shelter. Ryan saw grim faces everywhere and knew that everyone was feeling what he was feeling. *What if we blow it?*

"That's OK, we'll get them back," he said to Tracy. "We can score off their pitcher."

Tracy turned away without answering. He stalked off to the far end of the bench, where Art finally cornered him. "Your pitching form is fine, Tracy, and you've got plenty of speed on it. But, you know, your next meal doesn't depend on your striking out everyone. Relax, throw your best stuff, and if they can hit that, they deserve to win."

But at the bottom of the inning, Ryan was beginning to think the Jaguars did deserve to win. He buried his head in his hands as Brad watched a third strike go by. Something was wrong. Brad had never let a strike go by without swinging at it, especially not with two strikes on him. What was happening to the Braves? He looked down the row of faces to his left and could have sworn he was with a family that was watching their house burn down.

Art tried his best to shake the team out of their panic. "Hey, we're not playing the New York Yankees tonight! These are the Jaguars. You know, lovable little cats? We're here to play baseball, and you act like you're on deck for a Russian roulette match. The best effort I've seen tonight is when Mike chased that triple out into the weeds in left field."

If the Braves' batters were not getting the message, at

least Tracy appeared to have settled down. Although fighting another wild streak that caused him to walk four batters in the next two innings, he kept the Jaguars from scoring both times.

In the bottom of the third, Ryan finally got his first chance to bat. Suddenly he understood why all his teammates had been standing as if frozen in the batter's box. He was so desperate for his team to win that his arms were shaking and his spine was buzzing like a tuning fork. The first pitch came in waist-high and overly fast, but when he swung, he missed and nearly tripped over his own feet.

He gulped and glanced back at the bench. *May as well forget about a championship,* he thought. Then he caught sight of Art. The coach was smiling and holding his bat tightly under his chin.

"Ryan, if you squeeze that bat any harder you're going to leave fingerprints!"

Ryan backed out of the batter's box and looked at his hands. The knuckles were white as he clutched the bat. He grinned sheepishly at Art, dropped the bat, and shook both hands down at his sides.

"Just relax, Ryan, and I'll guarantee you an all-expenses-paid tour of the basepaths."

Ryan nodded and stepped back into the batter's box. Suddenly the bat didn't feel so heavy in his hands. It seemed to jump out at the next pitch, and sent the ball soaring into center field. Ryan had nearly reached first base when he saw that the ball would not be caught. He sprinted as hard as he could around the bases and did not even have to slide as he crossed home plate well ahead of the throw from the outfield.

"That's the spark we needed!" he heard Art saying as the team escorted their puffing catcher back to the bench. "Now listen to me, guys. Losing is no problem as long as you get beat despite your best effort. Don't beat yourself by worrying. Get loose out there."

Although the Jaguars scored another run in the fourth, Ryan could feel that things were turning in favor of the Braves. His teammates were talking, and diving for ground balls, and swinging at anything that came near the strike zone. Brad, Randy, and Tracy each hit doubles in the fifth inning as the Braves closed the gap to 7-5. Both the Braves and their parents were so caught up in the action that all were standing as the team came up for its final chance at bat. There was still tension in the air, but for Ryan it had changed from a stifling pressure to excitement.

Tracy led off with a hard-hit single to center field. Ryan and Mike jumped on top of the empty Braves' bench and cheered. Al then grounded out to first, moving Tracy to second base. But the lull in the Braves' celebration was quickly broken when first Dave and then Perry walked to load the bases. Ryan and Mike slapped hands atop the bench.

It was then that Ryan noticed Troy standing near Art and practically falling over him trying to get noticed, and it occurred to him that Troy hadn't gotten in the game yet. Every Brave had played in at least a few innings of every game before, and Ryan stopped in midyell as he tried to figure it out. This was a key game, and Troy was a good hitter. Did Art just get caught up in the excitement of the rally or did he know that Troy hadn't played yet?

Jimmy then swung at a pitch with two balls and no strikes on him and popped it up to third base. The Jaguars' third baseman grabbed it and reached over to tag Tracy, but Tracy had already scrambled back to the

90

base. The Braves' cheers stopped quickly as they realized they were down to one out and that Smith was due to bat.

Just then, Ryan figured out what had happened with Troy! Art had been saving him just in case he needed a good hitter in a tight spot at the end of the game.

"Hey, Troy can pinch-hit!" he said to Mike.

Both of them looked at Art, but the coach made no move to call Smith back from the on-deck circle. Mike jumped down and grabbed Art by the arm. "It's OK to pinch-hit this once," he pleaded. "Think about poor Smith. If he strikes out now, he'll feel worse than anyone. Do him a favor and let Troy pinch-hit for him."

Troy joined the small circle, and his wide eyes were doing a better job of begging than Mike was. Still Art seemed to be debating. Ryan knew what must be going on in Art's mind. He had never had anyone pinch-hit for someone else before. He had saved Troy for just such a moment, but now wasn't sure he could go through with it. He really didn't believe in it.

Ryan was torn. He hated to see Art default on his system of playing everyone equally, regardless of ability. But he wanted so badly to win.

Smith had almost reached the batter's box when Art finally tapped Troy's shoulder and nodded toward home plate. Smith wouldn't believe it at first when Troy grabbed his bat from him. He clung tightly to the bat and looked back at Art.

"Troy's up," said Art. "He hasn't been in all game."

Smith let go of the bat and stomped angrily back to the bench. *Cut out the act*, thought Ryan. *You're glad Troy is getting you out of a tough spot.*

Troy was so eager to hit that he chased an outside pitch and missed badly for strike one. But he caught the next pitch squarely and lined it just past the third baseman.

"Fair ball!" shouted the umpire. Tracy scored, then Perry, and finally, with a leap of joy, Dave soared high in the air and landed on home plate with both feet. He was quickly buried under a mob of Braves.

"What a game!" shouted Ryan from the bottom of the pile. "What a game!"

8
Blisters

The meal was never officially over at the Courts' house until the dishes were done. Danny was not much help; he usually created more of a mess than he cleaned up. So it was left to Ryan and his mom to wash whatever wouldn't go in the dishwasher.

Without even changing out of his Sunday clothes, Ryan ran the water into the sink and collected the dishes. As she always did when it was Ryan's turn to wash, Mrs. Court dipped a finger into the dishwater. Ryan had given up trying to make the water hot enough to suit her. In fact, he knew better than to let the water get too hot because his mom would automatically make it still hotter.

"Wasn't that Randy you were talking to in church today?" she asked as the steaming water streamed into the sink. "I don't think I've ever seen him in church before."

"He's been coming the last couple of weeks. His parents are thinking about joining the church."

"That's nice. You'll have to introduce me to them sometime. Are they switching over from another church?"

Ryan risked touching the water with his finger. Pulling it back quickly, he wondered how he was going to find the dishcloth under the suds without scalding himself. "No, they weren't going to any church. Randy's folks wouldn't go to one ever since his big sister had an accident riding her bike. She got hit by a car and can't use her legs at all."

"Oh, that's awful! I wonder what it was that changed their minds about coming to church, then."

"Randy thinks it had something to do with Art," Ryan said. "He was over to see them when Randy almost quit the team. I don't know, maybe they liked how friendly he was and how much he likes giving his time to other people and things like that. He's very active in a church across town, you know."

"Maybe they saw that it hadn't done them much good to be off to themselves for so long. Sometimes it takes a long time for the bitterness to go away," sighed Mrs. Court. "I remember how I felt when your father and I split up." She rubbed her cloth on a plate until long after it was dry. "But I do hope it turns out for the Olsons and they find what they need at our church. We should include them in our prayers tonight. You know, this coach of yours sounds like he's really something.'

"He is," agreed Ryan. "Best coach in the league. I've always liked playing baseball, but this has been the best year ever! Did you see that long article on him in the paper?"

"I'm afraid I missed it. Well, I can hardly wait to meet him. I am sorry, Ryan, that I haven't been to one of your games yet. I'll have to be sure and make it to this next one. When did you say it was? Monday?''

"Yeah. It's a big game, too!" said Ryan. The thought of the championship game got him so excited he no longer noticed the heat of the water as he scrubbed a frying pan. "You couldn't pick a better game to go to. We're playing the Hawks, and they're tied with us at 15 and 2. The winner gets first place and goes on to the regionals.''

"Oh, dear," frowned Mrs. Court. "I wish it wasn't one of those crucial games. You know how worked up I get watching these things even when they aren't for championships. It seems the game always gets close at the very end, and I get all caught up in it. I get so nervous I can't even watch and my stomach gets to be such a wreck I can't eat for days!"

Ryan grinned to think of his mom at the game. Her once-a-year appearance at his game was about the only time he ever saw her lose her cool. "We'll try to make it easier on you this year. Maybe we can get a big lead on them in the first inning. Then with Joe pitching you won't have to worry about the score, and you can sit back and enjoy the game.''

"I thought Tracy was your pitcher," she said, inspecting the frying pan in the sunlight and finding it clean.

"I told you about Joe and Tracy taking turns. Joe seems to get better every time he pitches. Did you know that he hasn't given up a run in his last two games? Even Tracy knows that Joe is the best pitcher on the team.''

"And how is Tracy living with that fact?"

"Oh, you know Tracy," shrugged Ryan. "He likes to be the best. I think it's bugging him so much that he's pitching worse instead of better. He talks mostly about his hitting these days. Of course, he keeps track of everyone's average and he's way at the top, hitting over .400.''

Mrs. Court didn't seem to be listening to Tracy's batting statistics. Instead she had pulled open a cupboard door and was peering at a calendar taped to the inside of it. ''Monday the 28th. No, I don't have a thing on for that evening. But what's this you've got on the 27th? I can't read your writing.''

Ryan shook the suds off his fingers and studied the calendar. ''That's the 'Walk for the Hungry.' Don't tell me you forgot about that, too!''

''As a matter of fact, I hadn't,'' she smiled. ''I was just wondering if you still planned to go on that.''

''Of course,'' Ryan said. ''Mike wants to go on it, too. Hey! You still haven't sponsored me yet. Can I put you down for ten cents a mile?''

''You mean I donate a dime for every mile you walk? How far is this? Thirty-one miles, I thought you said. Sure, I'll sponsor you, but what kind of shape are you going to be in for your game on Monday?''

Ryan unplugged the drain and thought a minute. ''I never realized the walk was the day before the game. Oh, it won't matter,'' he said, finally. ''I suppose my legs will get a little stiff but I'm not fast enough to steal bases anyway. And how much ground does a catcher have to cover?''

''I hope you know what you're getting into,'' said his mom. ''That thirty-one miles is nothing to sneeze at.''

''Can I go with Ryan on that walk?'' begged Danny, who had stopped running laps around the house long enough to see if there was any action he happened to be missing out on.

''No, you can't,'' said Mrs. Court. But as he charged

out the back door, she chuckled. "He would probably have less trouble than anyone. The way he goes around here, thirty miles would be a snap!"

Art Horton was the last person Ryan would have expected to throw his immediate future into confusion. And yet there he was, peeking out from beneath his car, with oil streaked on his forehead and dripping from his hand, and he was saying. "You're going to walk thirty-one miles the day before the Hawks game? Are you serious?"

Ryan tried to laugh off Art's reaction, even though he had biked over to the coach's house to make sure going on the walk was OK. "Come on, it's not a race. I can go as slow as I want."

"Have you ever walked that far before?" came Art's voice, echoing from under the station wagon.

"Well, no. Not that I ever kept track."

"I'm going to be honest with you, Ryan," said Art. "If you do go on that walk, you'd better plan to forget about playing on Monday."

Ryan couldn't believe his ears. What had happened to all Art's talk about not letting winning get in the way of life? Where was Art, the caring Christian? Ryan bent down to get a look at Art's face to see if he was really serious. As soon as he did so he nearly bumped into Art, who had finished changing the oil.

"You would bench me for that?" asked Ryan. "I thought you weren't big on a lot of training rules. Besides, some of the kids at our church have been planning on doing this walk for a long time. It's all set up. I thought you said we shouldn't be taking these games so seriously."

Art smiled and tried to rub an itch on his forehead

without getting more oil on his face. A fresh black streak over his left eye showed he wasn't successful. "Oh, I don't mean that I'm going to punish you for not saving your strength for the game. But I don't think you'll be physically able to play a hard-fought game the day after such a walk. You might, but I'm not at all sure. Could you hand me some of that paper toweling?"

Ryan tossed the roll of paper to him and leaned against the car. He hadn't thought going on the walk would be such a big deal. He tried to find out what Art really wanted. "So you don't think I should go?"

"Oh, no, I'm not making that decision for you," laughed Art. "That's up to you. What do you think you should do?"

"I wouldn't want to miss that Hawks game for anything."

"I wouldn't want you to, either. You're my only catcher."

"But still, I'd feel kind of funny about skipping out on the walk."

"Let's try to figure a way out of this, then," said Art. "How about if you sponsored someone else this year instead of walking?"

"I could," agreed Ryan. "But I'm kind of short on cash. I *do* have a decent pair of legs."

For the first time that Ryan could remember, Art seemed tired. He didn't bother to pick up the empty oil cans; instead he scraped them toward the garage wall with his foot. "I'm glad to see you're so concerned about this hunger thing. It's a Christ-like attitude, and I'm all in favor of that. I just wish the timing were better. You know *I* can sympathize with what you're doing, but the others are going to be much tougher on you if you can't answer the bell on Monday."

"You mean Tracy and the guys."

Art nodded. "They'll probably think that you're letting them down. Really, though, the one I'm worried about the most is you. You've worked as hard as anyone this season. I wish you could work something out so that you can do what you feel is your duty to this cause and still play against the Hawks. It's an experience I wouldn't want you to miss. Whether we win or lose, just to have played in a title game is an important moment."

A half hour before the Sunday starting time for the walk, Ryan was still mulling over his decision. Every time he thought his mind was made up, all the arguments against his decision rushed into his mind to tip the balance the other way. It was like leaning first one way and then another to keep a canoe from capsizing. It only rocked the boat even more. As usual, Ryan put off his final choice, hoping it would somehow take care of itself. He got home early from church and ate lunch by himself under the shade of a maple tree in the back yard. Already it felt so warm and humid that there seemed to be steam rising from the grass.

As much as Ryan admired Art as a coach, his warnings about going on the walk should have been enough to talk him out of it. Ryan felt surprised that Art hadn't been able to convince him. But there was something a little different about the way Art was acting. He was still pleasant and acted like he had all the time in the world to spend with each boy. But Art had said "my team" once when talking about the Braves in the past week. Maybe it was just a slip of the tongue, but it didn't sound like the same Art who had always played down his own importance to the team.

Ryan had almost talked himself into pulling out of the walk and sponsoring Mike, who didn't seem concerned about spoiling his chances in the Hawks game. After all, no one was counting on Mike to do much. But the thought kept coming back that the walk was important. Those Bible verses about feeding the hungry kept creeping into his mind, almost as irritating as a commercial that you can't stop humming. He remembered his mother encouraging him to stand up for what he felt was right.

"Ryan! Are you coming? We don't have much time!" It was Mike, his shoulders already shiny with sweat even though he was only dressed in shorts and a tank top. He sat on his bike, fanning himself with a fishing hat and holding sunglasses in his other hand.

Ryan found himself going the easiest way with his decision. Mike was urging him on, and Ryan was not set against the idea firmly enough to offer resistance. If he had really thought the walk would be that tough, he would probably have stayed away. But he had never been too tired for baseball in his life. He felt he could probably walk the thirty-one miles and still have the energy for a few innings before nightfall. *How tough can it be if you're only walking?* he thought.

Ryan had found out how tough the walk could be, and the ugly white bubbles swelling under the skin of his feet were lingering evidence. The late July sun had grilled the streets of Barnes City, and Ryan's feet had not been up to it. The lone pair of socks in his shoes had not been enough protection against blisters.

When he arrived for the Hawks game, Ryan was determined not to let on about his feet. As if the game weren't special enough, his mom had come and was sitting next to Troy's parents on the hillside. But not even the wads of cotton taped over his toes and feet could make the pain bearable when he walked. It felt like a dozen separate fires were burning on his shoes.

Gritting his teeth, Ryan tried to jog over to the first base sideline to help Joe warm up. He thought he detected Art studying him as he ran, and he gave an extra springy hop to show the coach that he had never felt better. He was glad his face was turned so Art could not see him wince when he landed. When he dropped into his catcher's crouch, he nearly fell over from the pain. Not only were his feet throbbing, but his legs were stiff and tender. Ryan saw Joe take deep breaths between pitches and thought, *I'll bet I'm the only one on the team who isn't thinking about the Hawks. Why did I ever go on that walk?*

Ryan knew that it was all over for him when he saw Brad approaching.

"I guess Art wants me to try catching for awhile," said Brad. "It sure wasn't my idea! You must be feeling pretty bad!"

Ryan handed him the mitt and tried to jog back to the bench. The sharp jabs of pain, however, made him struggle to keep up a good limp.

"How was the walk?" asked Art. "Look, I talked Brad into taking over the catching for today. You're in no condition for it. Come on and take your shoes off. There's no sense in making your feet worse than they already are."

Tracy and Smith were swinging bats, preparing to hit first, when they saw Ryan grimly unlacing his shoes. "What is this?" asked Tracy. "I thought you said you were feeling great!"

"Look at those feet!" Smith pointed. "You really must have ripped them up on that walk yesterday."

"You mean you went on that thirty-one mile thing the day before the championship?" asked Tracy. "I though you had more brains than that, Court. This is for the league title, you dope! You're just going to go give it to the Hawks!"

"Leave me alone," said Ryan bitterly.

Ryan was hoping Art would defend him, but only Mike hobbled over. "Hey, don't just pick on him. I went on that walk, too, and the same thing happened to me." From the way he walked it seemed his feet were just as bad as Ryan's, but Mike had not made any effort to hide the fact. In fact, he was so amazed at the size of his blisters that he could hardly keep quiet about them.

"*You* don't happen to be our only catcher," snapped Tracy, stepping back and swinging his bat. "You had to do something stupid! Way to go, Ryan!"

Despite Ryan's optimistic predictions to his mom, the Braves did not look like they were going to run away with the game. Even Tracy struck out in the first inning as the Braves failed to score. Fortunately, Joe was in top form and he fired the ball past most of the Hawks before they even swung.

Ryan did not feel like leading the cheers from his spot on the bench like Mike was. Instead he studied his replacement as catcher. Brad seemed to do fine—as long as the batters did not swing. But whenever the bat flashed across the plate, Brad shut his eyes, and the ball usually bounced all the way to the wire backstop. Brad must have been under orders not to even try to throw out baserunners. When the Hawks finally got a single, their player stole second and third base while Brad held the ball in his hand and stared at them.

One batter hit the bottom of the ball and lifted an easy pop-up right over home plate. Ryan jumped to his feet from force of habit. That ball would have been his to catch. But Brad had not seen where the ball went. He whipped his head from side to side searching for it, while it landed only two feet away from him, barely in foul territory.

"If it had been any closer it would have hit him," Mike muttered.

Ryan looked out to second base and saw Tracy squinting at him with his hands on his knees. Then Ryan turned away and scanned the hill for his mom. She caught sight of him and mouthed, "What's wrong?" Ryan pointed to his bandaged feet and his mom winced. Then she quickly looked away as Joe's next pitch came to the plate. The batter swung and missed, ending the inning and leaving the runner on third base. Ryan saw his mom's shoulders collapse in relief. *She really does get into the game,* he thought, *even when I'm not in it.*

Somehow Ryan wished it could be someone other than Tracy to get the Braves' first big hit. When the star player lashed a long double to score two runs in the fourth inning, Ryan was the only Brave who did not let out a whoop of triumph. He saved his applause for when Randy drove Tracy home with a single.

The 3 to 0 lead held up until the sixth inning. Suddenly Joe, who had been breezing through the Hawk lineup, ran into some problems. He walked the first batter, who then stole second. Then he followed with a pitch that seemed to float toward the plate at only half speed. The batter lined it past third base and sprinted around first and second bases. A run scored as the batter dove into third base, knocking down Perry, who was waiting for the throw from Smith.

"Come on, Joe!" shouted Ryan. The crowd behind the Hawks' bench suddenly came alive after several innings of frustrated silence. They shouted their encouragement to the next batter, a well-built, left-handed hitter whom Ryan recognized as the league leader in home runs.

Just as the batter stepped to the plate, Art called time-out and bolted to the mound. Ryan could hardly stand not knowing what they were saying; as catcher he was always a part of the conversations on the mound. He craned his neck, trying to see around Art's back to get Joe's reactions. Joe seemed to be pointing to a spot low on his back. Art nodded and rubbed the area for a few seconds, then patted him on the back and left.

Art's strategy was obvious from the first pitch. Brad stood up and moved far to the left of the plate while Joe went into his windup. Joe lobbed the pitch to Brad so far from the plate that the batter had no chance to swing.

"Intentional walk," nodded Mike, as Joe threw three more similar pitches. "With that good a hitter up, it was a good idea." The Hawk fans did not think so, and they booed loudly.

"I sure hope Joe can get us out of this mess," whispered Ryan. The pitcher seemed to be bearing down harder than ever, chewing furiously on his gum. With three balls and two strikes, Joe reared back and fired. Strike three!

"That's one out. Hang in there, Joe!" said Ryan. He glanced back on the hill and saw his poor mother clenching her fists so tightly he could almost see her knuckles turning white from where he sat.

Joe threw to the next batter, who swung and missed.

104

But Brad also missed the pitch, and the entire Hawk bench screamed, "Go! You can score!" Fortunately for the Braves, the runner on third hesitated. He started to sprint home, then stopped and finally scrambled back to third as Brad chased down the ball and threw to Joe covering home plate. The other Hawk runner had no trouble moving up to second base.

The players on both teams had barely settled back on their benches when the Hawks' batter hit a soft liner to Perry at third base. Perry jerked his glove up in front of his face and caught the ball. He then saw the Hawk runner scrambling to get back to the base and he touched the bag with his toe just ahead of the runner.

"Double play!" shouted Mike, and he ran to join the crowd of Braves who were hugging Perry and Joe.

"Hey! Come on, we've got one more inning to play, guys," warned Art. But he must not have been too worried about losing the lead, because he let Ryan bat in the seventh. Mike was offered a turn, too, but he claimed he could hardly stand up. Ryan was able to hit a ground ball to the shortstop, but was thrown out easily as he limped toward first base. It was the third out of the inning and Ryan returned to the bench while most of his teammates rushed out into the field. As Ryan sat, he was shocked to see Joe sitting next to him. A quick glance at the mound showed him there was no mistake; Tracy was getting ready to pitch the final inning.

"How come Art took you out and put *him* in to pitch?" said Ryan, barely masking his disgust for Tracy. He remembered each of Tracy's cutting remarks, word for word.

Joe didn't seem overly thrilled for a boy who had held the Hawks to one run through six innings. He stiffened his spine with a grimace. "Something's wrong with my back. I don't know; what does a pulled muscle feel like? Anyway, I started getting these pains in my back at the start of the last inning. Sometimes it really hurts to throw, like the time that guy hit a triple."

"What did Art say about it?" asked Ryan softly, eyeing his coach. Art was chattering constantly, trying to keep Tracy loose and build his confidence. It seemed as though the entire crowd sitting behind the Braves' bench was doing the same.

"He wanted to know if I could hang on and finish the inning. I told him I could try, and he said that if I could pitch out of trouble he would get Tracy to finish up, and we'd win the title."

"Well, you did your job. Great game!" Ryan told him, slapping him on the knee. "Thanks for getting me off the hook. If we'd lost because I couldn't catch, I don't know what I would have done."

"Thanks," shrugged Joe. "It wasn't your fault you got those blisters. Just one of those things."

"Come on, Tracy, fire at will!" shouted Art. "Don't worry about the hitters; they can't hit what they can't see! That's the way to dent your catcher's glove!"

Tracy seemed to be enjoying the role of relief pitcher. He was so confident on the mound, for a change, that he almost grinned while he pitched. A walk and a base hit made him a good deal more serious but the Hawks could not get another run across the plate. Tracy fielded the final ground ball and rushed over to first base to make the play himself.

It spoiled a moment that Ryan had been dreaming about for weeks. They were the champs, and were going on to the regionals. But Ryan shook Joe's hand and limped up the hill to talk to his mom. "Tracy, you hot dog!" he muttered to himself.

9
Tournament Game

Once the car left the Barnes City limits, Ryan hardly said a word. He sat in the back seat with Jimmy and Joe, each of them staring silently out of the windows. The front seat, meanwhile, was alive with chatter. Mike and his dad joined Brad in commenting on everything from the Hawks' game to the height of the cornstalks along the highway.

Ryan could not decide if he wanted the two-hour drive to Silver Heights to pass quickly or not. In a way, he could hardly wait to get his chance to represent Barnes City in the Region Six Tournament. It was an honor he had long dreamed of. But his dreams had always left out a few things. In them he had always been a hero, playing to the roar of the crowd and the crackle of a loudspeaker. Now he realized he had as good a chance for failure as success. *This really is the big time,* he thought. *What if it's too much and I play a bad game in front of everyone?*

One glance at Joe told him that his teammate was thinking the same thing. Joe's normally tanned skin seemed almost pale as he stared, unseeing, at the rows of corn rippling past his window. At one point Mr. Sherry caught sight of him in his rearview mirror and asked if he wanted him to stop the car for a minute. Joe shook his head.

They always say that it's the waiting that gets to you the most, Ryan thought as he turned back to his own window. *It's Tracy's turn to pitch this afternoon. Poor Joe is going to be a basket case by the time it's his turn tomorrow.*

The plain, black and white sign that announced "Silver Heights, population 19,200" sent a fresh current of tension through Ryan. Mike's dad slowed down and followed the two cars ahead of him as they snaked through the side streets on the west end of Silver Heights. There was another sign hanging on a wire mesh fence: "Silver Heights Municipal Field." Ryan fumbled with the door handle, got out of the car, and gawked. He had heard that Silver Heights had a great playing field for a town its size, and now he saw that it was true. There was a covered wooden grandstand, painted green, rising up from behind the backstop. About halfway along the basepaths, these stands gave way to bleachers. There were loudspeakers tucked into the corners of the roof over the center stands, and a large scoreboard loomed over the centerfield fence. A fence! Ryan grinned eagerly at the wooden boards, plastered with advertisements, that ringed the entire outfield. Never before had he played in an enclosed field.

As Ryan walked closer to the field, he marveled at the

basepaths, so smooth the dirt seemed to have been sifted and pressed down. The grass was thick and green, almost like a living room carpet with a well-groomed pitcher's mound in the middle of it. Then there were the foul lines marked off in white chalk. "This sure is the big time," whistled Ryan.

"I don't feel very good," he heard Joe say. "I hope Tracy can pitch both games."

"Come on, do you want to lose?" Ryan asked him. "We aren't going to the state tournament with Tracy pitching." He thought back to that morning, when the Braves had piled into the three cars for the trip. Tracy's dad had held his car door open for Ryan, but Ryan had refused the offer. He lied about having already promised Mike he would ride with him, and then had been relieved to find there was actually room for him in the Sherrys' car.

"But what if I blow it?" asked Joe. "What if—"

"Hey, none of that now," said Art, approaching and grabbing Joe around the shoulder. "You'll feel better once the game starts. Just relax. After all, you're probably the best pitcher in this tournament. Your opponents are the ones who should be worried about blowing it!"

After running his team through some fielding drills to get them used to the field, Art gathered his players in the dugout on the third base side. It was a real cement dugout with steps and a floor. Art sat on the top step, looking down at his players.

"Don't be psyched out by the field," he said. "It's a nice place, so I want you to enjoy it. But remember, it's still a ball field. Same shape, same size as what you usually play on."

"If you think this field is good, wait until we get to

state!'' said Tracy.

"I like your confidence, Tracy, but remember it won't be easy. I was talking to the sports editor of our newspaper, and he said that no team from Barnes City has gone to State for eleven years.''

"Twelve," corrected Tracy.

That little fact did not help Ryan's peace of mind.

"I've done some scouting over the past couple of weeks," Art continued. "From what I've been able to snoop out, the team from Crawford is far and away the best of the three other teams in the tournament. Don't start snickering at Crawford just because they're a small town. They play a pretty solid game of baseball. The other teams are from Silver Heights and from Storm-view. Now I've just been given the draw," he said, waving a small slip of paper, "and guess who we get in the first game?''

"Crawford," groaned a small chorus.

"Smile when you say that," Art grinned. "That's right, we get Crawford. What's the difference if we play them today or tomorrow? We're going to have to beat them to get to the state tournament. Now, since they seem to be the toughest opponent, we'll meet them with our toughest lineup. Over the last half of the season we did best with Joe as pitcher. This is no insult to you, Tracy, because you're a fine pitcher, but I think we should let Joe pitch against Crawford. You have to admit that Joe may be one of the top pitchers in this part of the state. We'll go with Tracy then in tomorrow's game.''

Tracy looked as though someone had just run off with his wallet. Ryan smiled to himself, because he knew that Tracy had told everyone he knew that he was going to pitch today. He had even talked some girls in-

110

to coming to Silver Heights to watch the game.

Joe, meanwhile, was stunned. Sweat broke out over his eyebrows, and he began fidgeting with his glove.

"Here's our lineup," Art said, unfolding another slip of paper from his hip pocket:

1.	Troy	first base
2.	Tracy	second base
3.	Ryan	catcher
4.	Randy	shortstop
5.	Brad	right field
6.	Perry	third base
7.	Al	center field
8.	Dave	left field
9.	Joe	pitcher

Ryan was mildly surprised that Art had again broken from his "no-favorites" system of lineups. Of course, it was a tournament. That made a difference. He was definitely glad Tracy wasn't pitching.

As Ryan walked along the fence to find a spot to help Joe warm up, he saw a long line of cars entering the parking lot. Fans were starting to fill the bleacher seats, and the public address system crackled as an unseen announcer began welcoming people to the game.

Ryan bent down about forty feet from Joe and held out his glove. He felt more confident about the game now that Art had put him at the heart of the batting order instead of in his usual ninth position. "Warm up slowly," he said. "Art says that when you've got so much nervous energy it's easy to start throwing too hard. Lob it in here, and save your fast stuff for the Crawford Colts."

After a few tosses Joe complained, "I don't know.

111

Something doesn't feel quite right."

"Don't start in on that," said Ryan. With his own nerves racing full speed he had little patience left for Joe. "Relax, will you? Just throw it like you usually do, and let the batters fall over themselves trying to hit it."

The Crawford Colts were to bat first, and Ryan took his position behind home plate. Nothing was second-rate at this field; the plate was shiny and the lines marking the batter's box were so white and clean that Ryan did not want to step on them. As the first Crawford batter was announced, the crowd began shouting, and Ryan's whole body felt numb with tension. He was glad he was facing the field and did not have to look at the crowd behind him.

"Stay loose, Joe!" Art shouted from the dugout steps. "I want you so loose that the flesh is just hanging from your bones. Don't clench that arm and get those muscles all tight. Ease up, leave your muscles free to work, and airmail that ball to home plate!"

The first Crawford batter was a small boy, and somehow that helped bolster Ryan's confidence. He crouched low, eagerly awaiting the pitch as Joe rocked back on his right leg and brought his arm forward. The ball rushed toward the plate and Ryan threw out his arm as the pitch sailed outside.

He returned the ball to Joe, who was shaking his head over something. Joe wound up and threw again. This time Ryan saw the bat nearly sweep over the plate and then pull back. "Steeeerike!" boomed the umpire.

The umpire was a large man with bushy eyebrows and a no-nonsense expression. He looked like he knew his business. Ryan flipped the ball back to Joe, who was still frowning despite the strike call.

The third pitch did not seem to be thrown very hard,

112

and the batter hit a sharp line drive to second base. Tracy took two quick steps and grabbed the ball across his left shoulder. He grinned, pulled the ball out of his glove and held it high for everyone to see. "See that, Joe, you got fielders today. Don't worry about those Colts."

The fielders had no chance on the next pitch as it seemed to jump off the bat into left field. *He pulled the ball to the left,* thought Ryan, staring at the Crawford player as he pulled up at first base. *What's wrong with Joe's fastball?*

The next batter fouled a pitch down the third base line and then doubled to left field.

"Come on, throw the ball! Don't lob it!" howled Tracy.

A terrible feeling was starting to come over Ryan as he watched Joe wind up. The pitcher was not rearing back all the way, and he held his arm close to his body, more like a shot-putter than a pitcher. The ball floated to the plate so easily that Ryan wanted to jump out and knock it away before the batter had a chance to swing. But the Crawford hitter waited for it and blasted it over the left field fence. He was still running the bases with the crowd cheering and the loudspeaker blaring out his name when Ryan went out to the mound. He felt his cheeks burning as he watched the batter touch home plate for the third run of the inning. Here they were, Barnes City champs, and they were being pushed around as if they had never won a game all year. All because Joe was scared out of his mind. Inside Ryan, all the tension about winning the tournament burst out in a flood.

"Look what you're doing, you chicken!" he snapped. "Would you just throw the ball? Just throw your normal speed and we might have a chance. And stop moping and wishing you didn't have to pitch today!''

Tracy had not bothered to join them on the mound, but he made his disgust known. ''You choker! You *would* fall apart in the big game!'' he shouted loudly enough for everyone to hear. Ryan heard Art shout at Tracy, telling him to knock it off.

It was as slow and painful a torture as Ryan had ever known. Joe walked the next batter and then gave up a long double, scoring a run. Finally Art ran out to the mound and Ryan jogged over to join him. He pulled a wet hand out of his catcher's mitt and dried it on his shirt.

''Chicken!'' spat Tracy, kicking the dirt by second base.

''Hey, what's wrong, pal?'' said Art. ''You're not throwing the way you have all year.''

Joe was trembling as he pounded the ball in his mitt, and Ryan saw his bottom lip quiver. ''It's my arm. I can't throw.''

''Excuses, excuses,'' muttered Ryan. ''Get Tracy in the game before they laugh us out of the ballpark.''

''Lay off, will you?'' snapped Art. ''What is it, Joe? You can't get loose? Sometimes it takes twice as long to get loose when you're nervous for a big game.''

''I don't know,'' Joe said. ''It hurts.''

Art frowned and sighed heavily. ''All right, take it easy on this batter. Throw four pitches way outside and throw them easy to see if we can't work the kinks out of your arm. Then pitch to the next batter and we'll see what happens.''

Joe followed instructions, but it did not seem to help. After giving up a walk, he had to dodge a line

114

drive that sailed past his shoulder and into center field for a hit.

Tracy was stomping around second base like an enraged rooster. "You're throwing like a girl! What is this? Big star chokes when the chips are down!" Art finally trudged out to the mound, flipped the ball to Tracy and escorted Joe back to the dugout.

Ryan watched in anger as many of the fans offered Joe polite applause for his effort. *As if he deserves that!* he thought.

By this time, Tracy felt angry enough to throw the ball through a wall. Although he was unusually wild and walked two batters, he escaped the inning with only one more Colt run crossing the plate.

No one coming off the field even approached Joe, who was slumped in the far corner of the dugout, his face buried in his hands. Art walked over to say a few words to him, but he did not respond, and Art finally went back to his position on the steps.

Ryan glared at Joe and threw off his chest protector. "What a baby!" he muttered. The game he had looked forward to for so long had turned into a nightmare before the first inning had been half over. Things did not get better as the afternoon wore on. Ryan struck out his first two times at bat. The Crawford pitcher was tall and thin and had an arm like a whip. It was bad enough that he could throw the ball so fast but he also had a sidearm motion that made the ball seem as if it were heading straight for the batter. Ryan had not even gotten a good swing during either of his strikeouts.

Even Tracy was called out on strikes, though he refused to accept the call. He stood on home plate, arguing that the pitch was low, until even the Braves were telling him to sit down and forget it. If Art had not finally come out and pulled Tracy away from the plate, the Braves' star would have been kicked out of the game.

Tracy may have been behaving poorly but even Ryan had to admit he was pitching one of his best games. Except for allowing two runs in the third inning, he kept the orange-capped Crawford team under control through six innings.

Ryan refused to talk to him or offer any encouragement, however. Ever since Tracy's remarks about the Walk for the Hungry, Ryan had decided he did not need a conceited show-off for a friend. He never visited the mound, and merely tossed the ball back to Tracy and waited for the next pitch. In a way, he was not sorry to see Tracy completely lose his cool. He knew how much Tracy had played this game up to his friends and how it must be tearing him apart to have his great Braves team look foolish in front of such a big crowd. *It's your own fault. You should keep your mouth shut once in a while,* thought Ryan.

The final straw for Tracy came in the seventh inning. He had been burning the ball in as hard as he could, walking two and striking out two. A Crawford player finally got a bat on the ball and hit a weak grounder to shortstop for what appeared to be the final out of the inning. But Randy kicked the ball, crawled after it, and then threw wildly trying to trap a runner off second base. By the time the ball was retrieved, two more runs were in. Tracy threw down his glove, walked over to Randy, and chewed him out. He paid no attention to Art's order to get back and pitch.

After all that, it was a relief to Ryan when Brad hit a high pop-up toward first base in the bottom of the seventh. The Crawford first baseman cruised under it, caught it, and jumped high in the air. The game was over with the score 9 to 2 in favor of the Crawford Colts. As he watched the celebration, Ryan decided that he had never spent a worse two hours in his life. From the first slow pitch to the last inning—in which the Colts had put in all their reserves—it had been embarrassing.

Many of the team's parents, as well as a group of the Colts themselves, were starting to mill around the dugout, trying to console the losing team. But after listening to a series of "Too bad it turned out that way" and "It was just one of those games," Ryan felt like screaming. He pulled off his Braves' shirt and replaced it with his blue windbreaker. He didn't want to be with the Braves or even be known as one of them at that moment. Everyone had seen what kind of a team the Braves were. The Braves were the team with the spoiled brat, Tracy, who had acted like a hotshot idiot in front of everyone. They were the team with the pitcher who panicked and could not have struck out anyone even if all the batters had been swinging pencils instead of bats. And they were the team that had managed only five hits and two runs off the Colts. One of those runs had been in the seventh inning when the Colts' top pitcher had left the game.

Ryan charged out of the dugout, but found an orange-trimmed uniform blocking his way. "Nice game," said the blond kid who had hit the home run in the first inning. "Too bad about your pitcher getting hurt. I think you guys could really have given us a close game."

Ryan allowed the boys to shake his limp hand, and then turned away. He pushed past some parents standing by the gate and went into the parking lot. "The pitcher was hurt, huh?" he scoffed. "Yeah, sure."

10
The
Phone Call

Never had a baseball game seemed so boring to Ryan. Art had insisted that, out of politeness, they should stay to watch the contest between Silver Heights and Stormview. They stayed and sat in a clump at the far end of the right field bleachers, but few of them actually watched the game. With their hopes of a championship dashed, they didn't care which team won. Ryan noticed that neither Art nor Joe was sitting with the team, and it bothered him that they'd gotten out of staying.

It seemed typical of the team's luck that day that the game went into extra innings. The Braves grew so eager to leave that they began cheering for whichever team was at bat to score the winning run. In the ninth inning, Stormview finally broke the tie and sent most of the hometown fans away disappointed in Silver Heights' 2-1 loss. As the Braves filed out of the stands, Art reappeared and asked to meet with the team in a corner of the parking lot.

Art told the glum group that they had nothing to be ashamed of. Most boys their age would have given much to have even made it to the regional championships. They had enjoyed a rare chance to play in a championship game and they had played hard.

"None of you backed away from the challenge," Art continued. Ryan was one of several boys who snorted and looked around to see where Joe was. Apparently he was still hiding somewhere.

"It was your coach who ruined your chances in this game." Ryan didn't believe he was serious till he saw that Art was looking into the eyes of each player. "I just got back from a clinic a few blocks away from here. They took a look at Joe, and it seems that he hurt his arm. It doesn't appear to be serious, but it was bad enough so that he shouldn't have pitched for at least four or five weeks. Now that was more than a bad break; it was bad coaching. The doctor thinks that he probably hurt it in the Hawks game. Remember when his back was bothering him and I left him in to finish the inning? It's very likely that Joe put some extra strain on his arm trying to compensate for his back pain.

"Of course, I was too blind to see this. To begin with, I should have recognized what had happened and gotten him out of that game as soon as he complained of the pain. I didn't, and the end result was that this turned out to be a rough game for all of us, especially Joe. I never thought I'd pull that kind of dumb stunt as coach. I tried to talk Joe into coming back with us to the motel, but he went back to Barnes City with his parents. He's taken this pretty hard, and the comments some of you guys made were pretty vicious. I don't know who was worse today, you or me!"

Ryan was stunned. He had not thought he could feel any worse than he had right after the game. But as Art's words sank in, and he thought back on the stinging accusations and taunts he had thrown at Joe, he felt even more like running away and screaming. He had thought that he was a Christian, that he was better than Tracy. Now he wished more than ever that they had never left Barnes City that morning.

It was to have been a special night. Some community groups in Barnes City had put up the money for them to stay overnight at the motel between the two days for championship play. It was a nice motel, and Ryan kept thinking about how fun it could have been to stay there. But after the disaster against the Colts, it only seemed like a place where the guys had to hang around together and kill time. No one looked forward to the meaningless third place game they were to play the next day against the Jets of Silver Heights.

Some of the players, led by Mike and Troy, tried to shake off their disappointment, and they jumped into the motel's heated swimming pool. Before long they had a rough game of keepaway going with a plastic football that Brad had brought.

But Ryan didn't feel like joining in. He walked out the front door and across the parking lot down to the end of the sidewalk. The sun had just set, the shadows were growing long, and the air was quickly turning cool. Ryan sat down where the concrete ended and a long row of evergreen shrubs began, and found the sidewalk still warm from when the sun had been out.

Ever since the team had left the park, he had been haunted by a picture in his mind of Joe sitting in the corner of the dugout. Those red eyes were looking toward the field, yet not focused on any of the action.

I really stuck it to Joe when he was down, thought Ryan. *I hate this whole day and this whole team.* He thought, bitterly, how easy it was to blame it all on one person. When he'd found out that Joe was not to blame, he had tried to work up a hatred of Art. After all, he was the one who had caused the trouble with Joe's arm. But it was not Art who said those things to Joe. No, Ryan Court had played a big role in the horrible things that had happened that afternoon.

"Mind if I join you for a few minutes?"

Ryan saw his coach standing in the shadows, stroking his mustache. *You picked a bad time for this. Leave me alone,* Ryan thought. But he said nothing, and Art's knees cracked as he bent down to sit beside Ryan.

"It's a good night for reflection," said Art. "No moon or stars to distract you." Ryan merely stared at his thumbnails, so Art went on. "It's been quite a year, wouldn't you say?"

"Yeah," Ryan answered wearily. "But something went wrong somewhere. We had it going so good, and then it all blew up on us."

"Well, that's what comes from inferior coaching. Here I spent all this time spouting off about playing the game the way it's meant to be played, and seeing that everyone gets something out of it. I said we weren't going to let winning control us. Then look what happened! I started letting all my principles slide. I guess I had forgotten how strong that urge is to grab first place. You start tasting a little success, and pretty soon all you can think about is more success."

There was a light shining on Art's mustache and it made the bristly hairs seem wilder than ever. Ryan shrugged and said, "It could happen to anyone."

"Well, I'm leading up to an apology, I guess." Art

121

smiled. "I started sacrificing players, looking for an edge, and now I wish I could step outside myself long enough to give me a good pounding. We really paid the price to win, but we didn't get anything for our money. Let me ask you: how much did you really enjoy that past couple of games?"

"I've had more fun at the dentist's office," Ryan said.

"I thought so. There was no sense of fun or joy. We lost our perspective on the game, and you can pin that on the coach."

"No, we're to blame for that, too," said Ryan. "We were talking all the time about going for the championship. You know, benching Smith and Mike and Justin against the Hawks. And all that stuff about going to State started with us. I never heard you talk about it."

"Well, we all got caught up in it. The point is, what can we learn from all this?"

"I know what I've learned," snorted Ryan. "I thought we were hot stuff, and now I know better."

"Don't be so hard on yourself, Ryan. You made a better effort to keep things in perspective than most of us did. I'm still kicking myself when I think of how little support I gave you when you went on the Walk for the Hungry. There you were, trying to do what you felt was right, and I gave out the impression that I thought a baseball game was more important."

A swarm of gnats suddenly hovered around Ryan's face, and he stood up to swat them away. "Well, whatever you did was nothing compared to what I said to Joe. I just can't believe I did that to a friend of mine."

Art did not reply for a moment. Then he said, "Do you think God knows anything about baseball?"

Startled, Ryan stared suspiciously down at Art. "What?"

"Just give me a few more minutes of your time and I'll be grateful," said Art, patting the sidewalk next to him. "When I was in college I also thought I was pretty hot stuff, as you called it. You know why I thought so? Because of this, right here." He held his right arm up for Ryan to inspect. "Can you believe it? I thought I was an important person because this arm could throw a ball faster than other arms could. I guess I thought that way until the day this arm broke down and couldn't throw hard anymore. There I was at age 19, washed up as a major league prospect. Yep, the scouts never looked at me after that.

"I had been counting on that arm to prove I was somebody, and when it failed me, I no longer had any proof. Ryan, I spent three years fooling around and getting myself in trouble because I thought I was a failure. I thought that until the day I walked into a church. There I talked with someone and found out that, even though I had given up on myself, God hadn't. He still cared."

Art seemed like a different person to Ryan. Maybe it was the weird combination of night lights and shadows, but as he watched Art, it seemed as though he had been introduced to him for the first time. He wasn't a flawless grownup. He was just another person, a friend with both strengths and problems. "Glad to hear it helped you, I guess," he said. "But what does that have to do with—"

Art held up a hand. "Just give me another minute. It takes a long time for thoughts to find their way out of this dense head of mine. I was going to say that, when I realized what I had done to the team today, and especially to Joe, I had that same low feeling. I felt like giving up. I had a perfect excuse, having just wrecked a season for thirteen great fellas. Fortunately, it didn't take me as long this time to figure out that God hasn't given up on me now, either. I spent some time talking to him about it. I still don't feel good about what I've done, and I may have some scars for awhile, but I think I'm ready to learn from what happened. I'll apologize to all the guys, and go on from there.''

Ryan felt himself wishing he could forgive himself the way Art had. ''Art, for you that's OK. You're a good person. But in my case you're not talking about a little slip-up or a wrong choice. I really came down hard on Joe—and I'm talking about mean, cruel stuff—when he was already down. The way I've been taught, that's the kind of stuff God really hates. I can say I'm sorry, but it doesn't change anything. You know what it would be like if I wanted to pray about it now? It would be like—like wrecking a guy's car and then asking him if you could borrow it again the next week.''

Art chuckled softly. ''I don't know. It seems like the best time to ask for help is when you're at your lowest.''

Ryan felt strange talking to Art about God. He did not really know him that well, and the only times he had ever spoken about religion were at church or at home with his mom. But somehow he did not quite want to let go of the subject yet.

''Don't you ever wonder what's the use?'' he said, looking Art in the eye for the first time. ''I really care about doing the right things, you know. Treating people right and all that. But it doesn't matter how hard I try. It often ends up like this. I either keep my mouth shut when I should speak up, or else I say something when I shouldn't.''

124

Art had a funny look in his eye, as though something had just occurred to him. "Ryan, do you remember back in our early practices when we had that system? When you weren't penalized if you swung at a ball in the strike zone, and when you got an out in the field if you so much as got your glove on the ball?"

Ryan nodded. He had almost forgotten about that time in the season.

"I really think God is the same way toward us," Art went on. "He doesn't expect perfection all the time. He wants us to try. Jesus wouldn't have had to save us if we could be perfect on our own. So I don't think God's Word is just a blueprint to show us where we've goofed. It's also like our practice drills, to get us thinking the right way about getting involved and trying."

Ryan thought hard for a moment, trying to connect everything Art was saying. "You mean what I did to Joe was like an error, a bad one? And God can forgive a Christian's errors—he just wants us to keep trying?"

Art shook his head in amusement. "Why is it that you can say better in two sentences what I've been rambling on about for five minutes? Well, I've imposed myself on you long enough. Brrrr! What's autumn doing here so soon? It's only the beginning of August." He rose to leave, but Ryan followed him in.

"The deal is, we're supposed to forgive other people's sins like God forgives ours, right?" Ryan continued as they entered the lobby. The shimmering light from the overhead chandelier nearly blinded him after the darkness outside.

"That the way I understand it."

"Well, I guess that's a start. Thanks, Art. By the way, have you seen Tracy lately?"

"He was in his room last I checked. See you later."

It was a good thing that the motel desk clerk had been willing to part with a fistful of change in exchange for their dollar bills. Neither Tracy nor Ryan had any idea how much a long-distance call to Barnes City would cost, and they were not taking any chances on coming up short. Between the two of them, Ryan figured, they now had enough change to play video games all night, but he wasn't interested in games now.

Tracy sat in the booth while Ryan stood in the doorway. The light over their heads was the only one turned on in the entire hall, except for the red exit signs on either end. Ryan had been surprised and relieved when Tracy volunteered to make the call. He did not like to talk on the phone, and thought he would blow the whole thing by forgetting exactly what to say.

While Tracy spoke with the operator, Ryan thought back to his resolution a half hour earlier after his talk with Art. Tracy had been on the bed in his room, watching tv when Ryan found him. It had not taken much to break the flimsy barrier between the two friends. All Ryan had said was, "You pitched a good game today. Best I've seen you throw all year. Too bad we didn't give you much support—especially me."

Tracy had responded more warmly than Ryan had expected. They both apologized for their behavior of the past weeks, and then Tracy explained the events behind his change in attitude.

"When I walked out of the dugout after the game, my dad was trying to cheer me up by telling me what a great game I'd pitched and how he'd never seen one team have so much bad luck in a game," Tracy had said. "But I was so mad I wasn't listening much to what he said. I was really teed off at Joe for his pitching, and at Randy for his error, and at that umpire and myself, too, for striking out.

"It was pretty crowded outside by then, and everyone was talking at once, so you couldn't hear much of what was said. But I heard some girls mention that number 12 on the Barnes City team. So I stopped to listen, and I heard them laughing about what a poor sport I was, and how everyone in the stands from Barnes City must have been embarrassed.

"I knew dad must have heard, but he didn't let on, and I realized that if everyone was talking about me now, it must have been worse during the game. Then none of my teammates were talking to me, especially not you, and suddenly I just wanted to dig a deep hole and jump in."

Ryan and Tracy had then talked about what they could do to make up for their remarks. Both had agreed that this phone call would be a good start.

Ryan could tell from the silence that Tracy was waiting for someone to pick up the ringing phone. His quick, deep breath gave Ryan warning that someone was home.

"Joe? Hi, this is Tracy. I called to, uh, apologize for that happened in the game today. Yeah. Ryan's sorry too. How's the arm? Well, keep soaking it, if that's what they said to do.

"Say, Joe, we really acted like creeps this afternoon, and we're sorry. We should have known something was wrong. I mean, when do ordinary humans pull the ball against a healthy Joe Martinez? Listen, the season isn't over. I know it's only for third place, but come on, a game's a game. We want you here. It's our last chance to get back on track as a team. Yeah, I know about your arm but we've got that figured out. Why don't you play first base tomorrow? That way you won't have to throw, and you can still get in the game. Ryan says he doesn't think Art will mind at all.

"What? So, maybe you'll make some errors. Who doesn't? You know Art doesn't ask for anything but a good effort and we know you always give that. Boy, do we know! Come on, get your dad to drive you back here tomorrow. The game is at noon."

A good effort is what God wants too, Ryan thought as Tracy hung up the receiver. He felt a little better already.

The Silver Heights stands were quite empty compared to the day before, and those fans who were there were lazily stretching out on the bleachers to enjoy the sunshine and the cool breeze. On one side of the field, the Silver Heights Jets, in their black and silver jerseys and caps, lifelessly tossed baseballs back and forth.

The Braves, meanwhile, huddled tightly in their dugout, and many of the Jets stopped to see what they were up to. Suddenly the team burst onto the field, carrying Joe above them. The mass of players cheered and escorted him to the infield, where the three boys who had been carrying him on their shoulders planted him on first base. As they clapped and whooped, a small segment of the Barnes City fans joined in with their applause.

Ryan trotted down the first base line toward home plate. Even if it was only a third place game, the field had been prepared flawlessly. He felt the smooth dirt of the base paths under his feet and it made him feel so light that he sprinted the rest of the way to the plate.

As he settled back in his crouch, the crisp lines of the batter's box brought back a few painful memories from the day before. But he looked out over at his teammates spreading out in the field. There was Joe, gritting his teeth as he concentrated on catching the practice throws from his teammates to first base. Smith was back in center field, pounding his glove and howling and watching his shoes settle into the lush outfield grass. Mike was on third base, gamely trying to get the best of a ground ball Joe had thrown to him. He knocked it down with his glove and crawled after it, then fired a high throw that Joe was barely able to flag down.

Tracy grinned at Ryan from the mound and asked if he was ready. After a few warm-ups, the rest of the Braves tossed their baseballs out of the field and started yelling encouragement to their pitcher.

"Go, Tracy!"

"Don't let us get bored out here. Give us something to catch!"

Ryan tossed the last warm-up pitch back to Tracy and nodded to the umpire. As the Jets' batter shuffled up to the plate, Ryan took a last look toward the dugout. Art was no longer on the step. In fact, he was sitting on the grass next to the fence with his hat off and a huge grin on his face.

"Hey! What a day!" he shouted. "Wish I was out there myself. Hey, Ryan, do you think I could pass for age twelve?"

"You'll have to shave off your mustache first!" Ryan shouted.

The Jets' batter stepped back and stared disbelievingly at the chattering infield surrounding him. He turned to Ryan and scoffed, "Don't you guys know this is only for third place? The game doesn't mean a thing."

Ryan grinned back at him. "Oh, yes it does!"